JUDI CURTIN grew up in Cork and now lives in Limerick where she is married with three children. Her first two books about Alice and Megan, *Alice Next Door* and *Alice Again*, are also published by The O'Brien Press.

Don't Ask Alice

Judi Curtin

Illustrations: Woody Fox

THE O'BRIEN PRESS
DUBLIN

First published 2007 by The O'Brien Press Ltd,
12 Terenure Road East, Rathgar, Dublin 6, Ireland.
Tel: +353 1 4923333; Fax: +353 1 4922777
E-mail: books@obrien.ie
Website: www.obrien.ie

ISBN: 978-1-84717-023-1

Cataloguing-in-Publication Data
Curtin, Judi
Don't ask Alice
1. Best friends - Juvenile fiction 2. Children's stories
I. Title II. Fox, Woody
823.9'2[J]

1 2 3 4 5 6 7 8

07 08 09 10 11 12

The O'Brien Press receives
assistance from

the arts
council
chomhairle
ealaíon

Illustrations: Woody Fox
Layout and design: The O'Brien Press Ltd
Printing: Cox & Wyman Ltd

For Dan, Brian, Ellen and Annie

Thanks to all my family and friends for their ongoing support.

Thanks to Ellen and Annie for their help with this book.

Thanks to everyone at The O'Brien Press, especially, once again, my editor Helen.

Thanks to Andrea and Robert for their hard work in the UK.

Thanks to all the schools, libraries and bookshops who invited me to read from the first two Alice books, and who unfailingly manage to round up groups of charming, interested children.

Thanks to everyone in third class in LSP who came up with such inventive book titles.

Thanks to all the kind children who have taken the trouble to let me know that they have enjoyed *Alice Next Door* and *Alice Again*. Special mention has to go to Sarah Holland who writes great letters.

Chapter one

Breakfast seemed to go on for ever and ever. The porridge burned and stuck to the pot in a revolting, stinky, sticky mess while Mum was listening to a 'really interesting' report about the environment on the radio.

'I could get a breakfast roll on the way to school, if you like,' I said.

Mum looked at me like I'd threatened to murder someone.

'Don't be ridiculous, Megan,' she said. 'Do you have any idea what goes into those breakfast rolls?'

I pretended to think.

'Rashers and sausages?' I suggested after a while.

Mum shook her head impatiently.

'Now you're just being silly,' she said. 'And it's so complicated, you'll be late for school if I try to explain. So you just sit there and I'll make some more porridge.'

I jiggled my spoon on the table impatiently while Mum slowly poured more oats and milk and water into a clean saucepan.

'It would be much easier to make porridge in a microwave,' I said. 'It only takes one minute, and it never gets burned.'

Mum stirred the porridge and ignored me.

'Oh, I forgot,' I continued. 'We can't make porridge in the microwave because we're the only people in the whole country who don't have one.'

Mum stopped what she was doing, and then there was a big row about all the possible ways microwaves might be rotting my brain. At that moment, I didn't really care if I got a rotten brain, just as long as I could finish breakfast and get out of there.

In the end I had to agree with Mum, just to keep her quiet.

After ages and ages, Mum put the bowl of porridge in front of me.

'One day you'll thank me,' she said.

I wasn't a bit sure about that, but I didn't want another argument, so I just smiled and said nothing. That seemed to suit Mum who hummed as she went back over to the sink and began to wash the porridge pots.

I ate the porridge so fast that I burned my tongue. Then I jumped up from the table, picked up my lunch and my schoolbag, kissed Mum and raced out the door before she knew what was happening.

*　　*　　*

For some people, this might have seemed like a

normal day – a day just like any other old day. It was the first day after the Easter holidays, I was going to call for my best friend Alice and we were going to walk to school together.

Big deal, you might think.

Walking to school with your friend?

What's so special about that?

But it *was* a big deal.

It was a very, very, very big deal.

You see, Alice had been away since September. She and her mum and her little brother Jamie had gone to live in Dublin, and for seven awful, never-ending months I'd had to walk to school on my own. Now Alice was back in Limerick, and I was so excited I could hardly breathe properly.

Luckily Alice had stayed with her dad that night, and he still lived next door to me. I don't think I'd have made it around the corner to her mum's fancy new apartment.

I knocked on her front door, and Alice

strolled out, just like it was any old day.

'Bye, Dad,' she called. 'Have a nice day at work.'

'Bye, Alice,' came her dad's voice from the kitchen.

Alice closed the front door behind her, and walked slowly down the path. Then all of a sudden she stopped, turned around, and raced back to where I was still standing on the doorstep. She gave me a huge hug.

'I can't believe it,' she said. 'I still can't really believe it. It is so, so, so, so, so, *so* fantastic to be back!'

I had to laugh. I knew Alice had missed me, but she would probably never have any idea just how much *I* had missed *her*.

And now that she was back, everything was going to be perfect.

Just like it used to be.

Chapter two

When we got to school, our friends Grace and Louise were waiting for us in the playground. We all hugged each other and then we got into a huddle and talked about what we'd done for our holidays. Grace, whose parents are really rich, had been to Lanzarote, and Louise had been to visit her cousins in Galway. I'd spent most of my holidays helping Mum in the garden. Would my friends be impressed if I said 'I planted six rows of carrots, and ten rows of cabbage and about a hundred rows of gross, disgusting parsnips?'

I don't *think* so.

So I stayed quiet, and no one noticed.

A few minutes later, Louise nudged the rest of us and hissed.

'Don't look now, but guess who's just walked in the gate.'

I didn't have to look. There was only one person in the whole school who we all hated. It had to be Melissa, the meanest girl in the world. Grace and Louise used to be friendly with her, but last year they had got sense, and now beautiful, blonde, horrible Melissa had to manage with only four people who thought she was the greatest thing ever.

I turned around and watched as Melissa kind of glided across the yard. She was wearing a totally cool new denim jacket, and she kept tossing her hair like someone in an ad for shampoo.

Already her four best friends were fluttering around her like over-excited butterflies.

Alice laughed.

'Same old Melissa. I bet she's really looking forward to seeing me again. What did she say when she heard I was coming back?'

Grace, Louise and I looked at each other and grinned. This was going to be *so* much fun.

'We didn't tell her,' I said.

'We thought we'd surprise her,' added Louise.

Alice grinned, and kind of slipped in behind Grace, who's really tall. I knew this was going to be great. Alice was always the only one in our class who could really stand up to Melissa and her mean ways, and Melissa was going to be *so* sorry to see her again.

Melissa was getting close. She looked at Louise first.

'Ever hear of a hair-straightener?' she said.

That was really mean, because Louise *hates* her curly hair. Louise went red, but before she could say anything, Melissa turned to me.

'Hi Megan, did you have a nice holiday? Or did you and your super-cool mum with the lovely *fashionable* clothes spend your time saving the planet for the rest of us?'

Melissa's friends giggled like this was the funniest thing they'd heard in their whole lives.

Usually it makes me really mad when Melissa mocks my mum, but this time I didn't care. I didn't reply. Nothing Melissa said could hurt me now.

Just then Alice stepped out from behind Grace.

'Hi Melissa,' she said. 'So nice to see you again. What did you do for your Easter holidays? Pick on people? Kick grannies in the shins? Steal sweets from babies?'

Melissa stopped her hand in the middle of a hair-flick.

'Alice?' she whispered, like a character in a film who's just seen the person who has sworn to kill them.

Alice grinned cheerfully. 'That's me – got it in one.'

All the colour had drained from Melissa's face, making her even paler than usual.

'What… what… what are you doing here?'

'Same as you, I expect. I came to get an education,' said Alice.

'But… but… '

Grace, Louise and I started to laugh. Melissa was always so cool and so confident; it was great to see her lost for words.

She tried again.

'But… you… I … mean… don't you live in Dublin?'

Alice grinned again,

'Well, I did move to Dublin, but I missed you so much I decided to come back.'

Suddenly Melissa relaxed a bit,

'Oh, I see. You're just back for a visit.'

Alice thought for a second,

'I suppose you could say that. It's just that it's

going to be a very long visit. I plan to stay here in Limerick for the rest of my life.'

Melissa looked like she was going to throw up all over her fancy new pink sandals. Just then the bell rang, and the rest of us ran into school. Now that Alice was back, school was going to be fun again. I just knew it.

Chapter three

The next few weeks were great. Some mornings I called for Alice at her dad's place, and other mornings I picked her up from her mum's place. At first it seemed a bit weird, but soon it just seemed normal, and it was hard to remember a time when her family had all lived together in one house.

The whole class was getting really excited because our Confirmation was coming up. We did hardly any real work. Most days we went to the church and practised hymns, and stupid stuff like getting in and out of our seats, and walking to the altar in neat lines. At first it was really hard, and people kept ending up in the wrong places, and our teacher, Miss O'Herlihy, kept saying stuff like, 'What are we going to do when the bishop is here?' and 'You're going to make a holy show of me!' After a while though, it got so easy we could do it in our sleep, and it was really boring, but as Alice said, anything was better than maths.

At lunchtimes, we mostly talked about what we were going to wear for our Confirmation. Melissa told anyone who would listen that she was going to Arnott's in Dublin to buy a designer dress and matching high-heeled shoes. Grace was actually flying to London to buy an outfit, but that didn't seem as bad because she didn't keep going on and on about it.

I didn't say much during these conversations. I never, ever have cool clothes. If it was up to

Mum, she'd knit me a Confirmation dress, or weave it from twigs and leaves or something. Whenever I mentioned Confirmation clothes to Mum she just said,

'Stop fussing – it's ages away. And Confirmation is a religious occasion – it isn't just about the clothes you know.'

I knew it wasn't just about the clothes, but it might as well be. If I had to wear something totally gross, Melissa would probably laugh out loud when she saw me, and the whole day would be ruined.

So one Saturday, I got up really early and did loads of jobs before Mum and Dad got up. Then I brought them their breakfast in bed. (I even made porridge to get Mum in a good mood.)

My little sister Rosie was already in Mum and Dad's bed, all curled up like a baby. Dad laughed when he saw me coming into their room with the cups and bowls rattling on the tray.

'What's all this about, Megan?' he said. 'I

suppose you want something.'

I nodded. No point pretending – Mum and Dad could always see through me anyway.

I took a deep breath.

'Please, please, please can we go and buy me Confirmation clothes today? Everyone else has theirs already, and if I don't get something soon everyone's going to think I'm a total loser.'

Mum sat up in bed so I was able to get a good look at her nightie, which was all faded and about a hundred years old.

'Don't be so dramatic, Megan,' she said, 'And I've told you before, anyone who judges you by your clothes doesn't deserve to be your friend.'

I sighed.

'OK,' I said, 'Forget the loser thing. But *please*, Mum, will you take me in to town today to buy new clothes?'

Mum thought for a minute.

'Actually,' she said, 'I was thinking of tidying out the garden shed today. I thought you might help me. You could—'

Dad interrupted her.

'Go on, Sheila. Put the poor girl out of her misery. I'll take Rosie to the park, and you two can go shopping.'

As soon as he said this, Rosie popped up her head and said,

'Yay! We're going to the park,'

and everyone laughed – especially me.

* * *

An hour later we were in town, and after I'd managed to steer Mum away from the charity shops and the horrible shops that sold grey, hairy, tweedy stuff for grannies, we did OK.

I ended up with really cool white trousers, a blue and white stripy top, and a loose white shirt to wear over it.

On the way back to the car, I was so happy I felt like singing. The impossible had just happened – I was actually going to look normal on my Confirmation day.

Then I had a totally scary thought.

What was Mum going to wear for my big day?

I had to know, but at the same time, I reeeeally didn't want to know.

This could be a complete disaster.

How would anyone even notice my cool new clothes if Mum was there beside me looking like a weirdo from the dark ages?

'Er, Mum,' I said, 'Are you getting something new to wear for my Confirmation?'

She tossed her crazy hair back from her face, and laughed like I'd just told the funniest joke in the world.

'What a thought!' she said. 'Sure, haven't I a wardrobe full of clothes at home?'

It was true, she did have a wardrobe full of clothes at home. A wardrobe full of ancient, ugly and totally embarrassing clothes. A wardrobe full of clothes that looked like they belonged in a museum.

While I was still getting over the shock of

Mum wearing her old clothes to my Confirmation, she continued,

'Actually, if I work really hard I could finish the jumper I've been knitting for myself. That would be nice, wouldn't it?'

I gasped.

Surely she was joking?

She *had* to be joking.

Mum had been knitting this jumper for about two years. It was a huge, shapeless thing, made out of odd scraps of wool left over from other ugly knitting projects. It was a disgusting mixture of orange, red, pink, brown, purple and gross, slimy green. It was as if all the horrible jumpers Mum made me wear when I was small had come back to haunt me. If Mum finished this jumper and wore it to my Confirmation, I might as well just give up forever. I might as well go to the ceremony with the word 'loser' tattooed in capital letters right across my forehead.

I stopped walking.

'I know your jumper is going to be beautiful,' I lied, 'But why don't we go and buy you something new. You deserve it.'

Mum smiled.

'Thanks love, but if I'm getting something new for myself, I'd prefer a new juice extractor, or maybe a nice new pair of gardening gloves. Still though, it's very kind of you to suggest it. You're a very thoughtful girl, Megan.'

Then, right in the middle of the street, she turned and hugged me. I wriggled free as soon as I could. It was bad enough being seen in town with my mum. If anyone saw her hugging me, my life was over.

Mum didn't even notice how embarrassed I was. She just walked on, muttering to herself.

'Now, if I work hard, I can finish the left sleeve tonight. I can join in some of that lovely yellow wool from that cardigan I made for Rosie last year, and maybe some of the brown too.'

I felt like throwing myself onto the footpath

and crying my eyes out.

I was doomed.

It would take a miracle to get my mum into some decent clothes.

*   *   *

A few days later, the miracle happened.

Dad came home from work waving an envelope over his head. He actually skipped into the kitchen. I'd have been embarrassed if I wasn't laughing so much.

'I won a prize in the office raffle,' he said. 'It's the first time I've won in twenty years.'

Mum ran over and tried to grab the envelope from him. (She loves getting stuff for nothing.)

'What is it, Donal?' she said. 'What did you win? Is it the voucher for the pellet stove? Or the gardening weekend? I'd just love to go on a gardening weekend.'

Dad shook his head.

'Sorry, love. It isn't any of those. It's a voucher for a clothes shop.'

He opened the envelope and read,

'O'Donnell's on Catherine Street. Two hundred and fifty euro. Not bad, eh?'

Mum sighed. 'Two hundred and fifty euro on clothes. That's an obscene amount. I wouldn't spend that in twenty years.'

She was right. Most of the clothes Mum wore cost fifty cent in the charity shop bargain bin. When she got married she borrowed her wedding dress from a friend of her granny's. Why couldn't she be more like Alice's mum, Veronica, who could spend two hundred and fifty euro on clothes in her coffee break?

I leaned over Dad's shoulder and looked at the voucher. I didn't dare to touch it – it was much too precious for that.

'Look,' I said to Mum, 'You have to spend it within three months. So you might as well ... buy something new for my Confirmation.'

Mum sighed.

'But what about my jumper? I only have half a

sleeve left to knit, and I have some really nice colours I want to add in. There's a gorgeous purple I want to use.'

Dad saw the look of horror on my face. He winked at me, and patted Mum's arm.

'You know what the church is like on Confirmation day, Sheila. It's always crowded, and it'll be far too warm for you to wear your jumper. Why don't you save it for Christmas? Meg is right. Use the voucher and buy something new.'

Mum nodded slowly.

'I suppose you're right. And it would be a sin to waste your prize.'

I raced over and hugged Dad until he begged for mercy.

*   *   *

So next day, Mum, Rosie and I went to O'Donnell's to buy the new outfit. The lady in there was really nice, and helped us pick out a lovely pale green dress and jacket. When Mum came out of the changing room, Rosie stared at her, and rubbed the dress and said,

'You look pretty, Mummy!'

Mum gave a kind of shy smile, and for once in her life she really did look pretty.

The only bad moment was when the lady said that once Mum's hair was blow-dried she'd look perfect, and that we all had bad hair days, didn't we? Mum went as red as the hem of her almost finished jumper. I knew why. The lady was trying to be kind, but how could she know that Mum's hair was always like this – all scraggy and wiry like the scourer we use for washing really dirty pots? How could she know that Mum hadn't had her hair blow-dried since she was about fifteen?

The lady looked at Mum's red face, and realised her mistake. She leaned over and pulled a beautiful floaty scarf from a display. She swirled it around Mum's neck.

'Here,' she said, 'Let's throw this in as a little extra – a present from us. It finishes off the outfit just perfectly.'

Mum smiled at her, and went to change back into her dungarees.

A few minutes later, she handed over the voucher, and I dragged her home before she could change her mind.

That night, for the first time ever, I dreamed that I came from a normal family.

Chapter four

The morning of my Confirmation was lovely and sunny, so we walked to the church. I don't like walking all that much, but at least it meant that horrible Melissa wouldn't get to see our old, battered car.

I felt really good in my new clothes. I couldn't remember the last time I'd had all new clothes in one go.

Mum's dress made her look kind of young and mysterious, and she had let me tie up her hair with one of my nice clips, so she didn't look like a jungle-monster any more. Dad had his best suit on, and Rosie looked cute in a pretty pink dress that used to belong to our cousin in Cork. So we all strolled along, and I felt really happy with my maybe-not-so-crazy-after-all-family.

When we got to the churchyard, Alice raced over and hugged me. I hugged her back. I was so, so glad that she was there, making her Confirmation with me, instead of making it in Dublin with a big load of strangers.

'Megan,' she screeched, like she hadn't seen me just the day before. 'Happy Confirmation day. You look fab. I love that shirt. And your Mum looks double-fab.'

Rosie came over with her thumb in her mouth.

'What 'bout me?' she asked.

Alice picked her up and swung her around in the air.

'You look fabbest of all,' she said, and Rosie put her arms around Alice and gave her one of her special hugs.

Just then Melissa walked past. She had a long, slow look at me and my family, and I could see that it made her really crazy that she couldn't find anything to mock.

I thought Melissa looked totally disgusting. Her super-fancy dress from Dublin was too sparkly and glittery, and she wasn't able to walk properly in her high heels. Her hair was piled up on top of her head in a complicated heap of curls and swirls that looked a bit stupid. (And I couldn't help hoping that a sudden gust of wind would come and mess it all up.)

Melissa's big sister was wearing an ugly long black dress, with huge safety pins stuck all around the sleeves. Her black lipstick made her look like someone who'd escaped from a vampire movie.

Melissa's parents looked all stiff and starchy,

like they were going to dinner with the president or something.

I could have mocked Melissa and her family, but I didn't. I felt too happy.

Soon Miss O'Herlihy came along, and rushed us into the church, and into our seats.

I knew Mum was right – Confirmation isn't about the clothes, but I was so happy not to be a freak for once, I said an extra prayer of thanks in my head.

* * *

After the ceremony, we all went across to our school for a little party. Alice, Grace, Louise and I sat on a windowsill, and drank bottles of orange and ate biscuits, and checked out what everyone was wearing.

When it was time to leave, my family had to go and visit loads of boring relations. I'd have pre-ferred a big party with one of those huge, bouncy slide-things, but unfortunately Mum had only got a new dress, not that personality transplant I'd been dreaming of.

Later that evening we went out for dinner with Alice's family. Alice's mum, Veronica, and my mum wouldn't exactly be friends, but we had bullied them into the idea of a joint Confirmation dinner. Alice's mum agreed because otherwise it would have just been her, Alice's dad, Peter, Alice and her brother Jamie, and that might have been a bit embarrassing. I still don't know why my mum agreed. She'd have preferred a bean curry and brown rice at home.

Anyway, I didn't care, the restaurant was booked, and Mum couldn't back out, even if she wanted to.

We had a really nice time at the restaurant. Alice and I sat next to each other and chatted about our day. Jamie, who used to be really bold, was very good and he and Rosie coloured in about a hundred pictures together.

Dad and Peter talked about soccer, just like they always did.

Mum and Veronica tried really hard. Mum hardly mentioned the environment at all, and Veronica only mentioned shoes twice and hand-bags three times.

At the end of the evening we all stood out in the street and said goodbye to each other. Veronica even gave Peter a kiss on the cheek before she left with Alice and Jamie.

I gave a little sigh of happiness. Now every-thing was OK. I was sure of it. Alice's parents were still separated, but at least they were being sensible about it. Now, I decided, Alice would be able to accept that her parents' relationship was over forever. Now she could put all of her plot-ting and scheming behind her. Now we could concentrate on enjoying our last few months in sixth class.

I should have known better.

Chapter five

Next morning, Alice called over while I was still in my pyjamas. Mum let her in, and she came to my room and sat on the bed. She didn't say anything. When Alice was quiet it was usually time to get worried. I looked at her carefully.

'Everything OK?' I asked.

She shrugged.

'S'pose so.'

'Yesterday was great, wasn't it?' I said.

'S'pose so.'

'And didn't Melissa look totally stupid in that dress?'

'S'pose so.'

'And what about that crazy hairdo she had? Bet it didn't last the whole day.'

'S'pose so.'

I waited, but Alice didn't seem to have anything else to say.

I grabbed my clothes and went to take a shower. When I came back, a few minutes later, Alice was still sitting in the same place. I was starting to feel nervous, so I tried again to make conversation.

'Remember when you hid in this room that time last year, to try to make your mum come back to Limerick? That was really funny, wasn't it? I can't believe you stayed in here for so long …'

Alice nodded, but she didn't laugh like she usually did.

I sat beside her, and shook her arm.

'Come on, Al,' I said. 'It's me – Megan. Tell me. What's going on?'

Alice gave a big, long sigh.

'It's Mum and Dad.'

I shouldn't really have been surprised. Since Veronica and Peter had split up, Alice had been really mixed up. It had been stupid of me to think that everything was all right, just because Alice was back living in Limerick again.

'What about your mum and dad?' I asked.

'Well, remember I told you before that I knew they'd never get back together?'

I nodded, and she continued,

'I've changed my mind. I think maybe they could get together again. It's stupid for them to go on living like this.'

I wasn't sure what to say to this, so Alice kept talking,

'You were there yesterday – you saw them. They were like best friends.'

This wasn't really true. What really happened was that for the first time in years, they hadn't sounded like total enemies. I knew I couldn't say that to Alice though, so I said nothing.

Alice sat in silence for a minute then she jumped up as if we hadn't just had that conversation.

'Come on,' she said. 'Let's play Swingball. Best of five games. Bet I beat you.'

I got up and followed her into the garden, glad that the awkward moment had passed, and that Alice was back to her normal self.

Once again, I should have known better.

The first sign of something strange going on was that I actually beat Alice at Swingball, something I hadn't done since the time we were six years old and Alice was playing with a broken right arm. I was glad I had won, but it didn't feel right somehow – like Alice hadn't really been trying.

We went and sat in Rosie's playhouse. Alice

grabbed my arm, and said, 'Megan,' in a real breathless kind of way. I looked at her, and saw a funny glint in her eye. It was the old glint that always made me very scared. The glint that meant she was plotting and scheming again. The glint that always led to trouble in the end.

I knew there was nothing I could do.

'What?' I said, trying not to sound as nervous as I felt.

Alice grinned at me.

'I think it's time Dad got a girlfriend.'

Hello?

Where had that come from?

Maybe I hadn't heard her properly.

'Pardon?'

She spoke slowly and clearly.

'I said, I think it's time Dad got a girlfriend.'

I wondered if she'd hit her head with the Swingball bat or something.

I folded my arms and looked her in the eye, and tried not to notice the funny glint.

'Alice O'Rourke,' I said. 'What are you on? When you thought your mum had a boyfriend you nearly lost it. And a few minutes ago you said you thought your parents should get back together, so why on earth do you think your dad should get a girlfriend?'

She grinned at me.

'You're a clever girl, Megan. You're so clever you can do long multiplication without a calculator. You go figure it out.'

I tried to figure it out. Really I did. But it was hard to think straight because all I knew for sure was that Alice was up to something, and that, before too long I was going to find myself right up to my neck in her crazy plan.

After a minute I looked up at her.

'I give up. This is harder than long multiplication. This is even harder than long division. You're going to have to tell me – why should your dad get a girlfriend?'

Alice smiled at me

'Because it would make Mum jealous.'

I still didn't understand.

Alice continued,

'You know what Dad's like. He's always there. Always available. He's like an old pair of jeans that you're comfortable in, but don't think about very much. If Dad suddenly got interested in someone else, it might make Mum pay a bit more attention to him. She might realise that leaving him was a mistake after all.'

I put my hands over my face. It did make sense – in a crazy kind of way. I didn't want to admit this to Alice, though. I didn't want to encourage her. I tried to sound casual.

'Even if a girlfriend for your dad was a good idea. Where do you think this girlfriend is going to come from? Girlfriends don't grow on trees you know. And last time I checked you couldn't buy them on eBay.'

Alice sighed.

'Ha, ha! Very funny. *Not*. Know what, Megan?

You always make everything sound difficult.'

I laughed.

'That's only because you make everything sound so easy.'

I was glad to see that she grinned back at me. Maybe there was hope for her yet.

Just then Mum called from the back door.

'Megan, Alice, come on in. I've made you some delicious carrot and apple juice.'

Alice and I made faces at each other and got up to go inside. I knew the matter wasn't finished with though.

I knew that Alice was just revving up for another one of her crazy plans.

Chapter six

When I called for Alice the next morning she didn't mention her mum, or her dad, or anything about girlfriends or secret plans. By the time we got to school, I was beginning to relax.

Maybe Alice had got sense overnight, I thought.

Maybe we could spend the next few weeks just enjoying ourselves.

And maybe one day, purple and yellow stripy pigs will fly past my bedroom window singing '*Oops I did it again*'.

*   *   *

At lunchtime, just when I was looking forward to the two of us hanging out with Grace and Louise and swapping Confirmation stories, Alice dragged me off to a corner of the playground, away from everyone else. She pulled me behind a shed, and said in a real dramatic voice – 'Miss O'Herlihy.'

I had no idea what she was on about.

'What about Miss O'Herlihy?

'She's perfect.'

I didn't say anything. Since when was Alice so interested in teachers?

Alice poked me in the arm.

'Well?' she said. 'What do you think, Meg? Isn't Miss O'Herlihy just totally perfect?'

I shrugged.

'Well she's OK, I suppose – for a teacher. But I

wouldn't exactly say she's perfect. Remember that maths test last week? She marked two of my sums wrong even though they were right. And before Christmas she got really cross with Grace over something that wasn't her fault at all. And—'

Alice interrupted me.

'Pay attention, Dork-head. I don't mean Miss O'Herlihy is perfect as a *teacher*. I mean she'd be a perfect girlfriend for Dad.'

I don't like Alice calling me Dork-head (well, I suppose I don't like anyone calling me Dork-head), but I decided to ignore it – I had more important things on my mind.

'But Miss O'Herlihy is a teacher.'
Alice looked at me like I was totally stupid.

'Well, duh. I *had* noticed that,' she said. 'But teachers are people too.'

I couldn't believe what I was hearing.

'But your dad, and Miss O'Herlihy, that's like…. it's…. I mean… that's just gross.'

Alice folded her arms.

'No it's not. And anyway, I don't want them to fall in love or anything. I'd just like it if they went out together once or twice. Just long enough for Mum to find out, and hopefully get a bit worried.'

This was starting to make sense, and I really didn't want that. It was all too weird for me. I decided to change direction.

'Miss O'Herlihy probably has a boyfriend already.'

Alice shook her head.

'Nah. Doubt it. If she did she wouldn't stay so late after school. She'd be rushing home to get ready for dates and stuff.'

I wasn't sure if Alice was right or not. All I knew was that if she tried to get her dad to go out with Miss O'Herlihy, things could turn very nasty. And I *so* did not want to be involved when it happened.

Alice giggled suddenly.

'I know exactly what I'm going to do. It's simple.'

I sighed. Alice didn't seem to know the meaning of the word 'simple'.

Alice went on,

'I'm going to be so bold this afternoon, that Miss O'Herlihy will have to send for my parents. I'll fix it so only Dad comes in, and—'

I interrupted her, '—and your dad will say, "Thanks for telling me that my daughter is the boldest girl you've ever taught, and by the way, you've got beautiful eyes and what a pretty dress you're wearing today and will you go out with me?" I don't know, Al. Maybe it's just me, but I can't see that plan working very well.'

Alice stamped her foot.

'OK, Smarty-Pants, so it's not the best plan ever. It's just the best plan I can think of right now. Can you do any better?'

I sighed again. I *sooo* did not want to be involved, but I couldn't let Alice continue with this stupid plan. After my trip to Dublin at mid-term, I knew exactly how bold Alice could be – and it wasn't pretty. She'd just end up in loads and loads of trouble. And Miss O'Herlihy wouldn't send for her dad anyway. She never did stuff like that. She'd probably think of a totally disastrous punishment, like banning Alice from our graduation party or something.

Alice stamped her foot again. I wondered if I should tell her that stamping your foot is a bit immature for someone who will be going to secondary school in a few months time. Even Rosie doesn't stamp her foot any more, and she's only four.

Alice seemed to be waiting for an answer.

'Well?' she said.

I didn't know what to say, so I said nothing.

Alice folded her arms and looked at me carefully.

'OK,' she said. 'You've got twenty-four hours to think of a way of getting Dad together with

Miss O'Herlihy, and if you can't think of anything, I go back to plan A, and do something really bold.'

Now what was I supposed to do?

This was awful. Just when everything seemed to be going so well, Alice had to start plotting and scheming again. I felt sorry for her, really I did. I knew it couldn't be much fun having your parents separated. I so wished that life around Alice could be simple again – just like it used to be.

The bell for end of lunchtime rang, and for once in my life, I was really glad to hear it. I started to walk towards our classroom. Alice raced after me, and grabbed my arm.

'Twenty-four hours. OK?'

I nodded slowly.

'OK.'

What else could I say?

Chapter seven

Twenty-four hours later, Alice and I were back in the same corner of the playground, behind the same shed. I felt like one of the lead characters in a very bad movie.

'Well,' she said, 'Let's hear your great plan.'

I played for time.

'How do you know I have a great plan?'

She laughed.

'I know you won't let me down. You never let me down. You're my very best friend.'

Sometimes being Alice's best friend seemed like a very big responsibility, and an awful lot of hard work. I'd hardly slept the night before, racking my brains for a good plan. In the end, the plan I came up with wasn't really that good at all. It was just OK, but at least it was better than Alice's stupid idea.

Alice was waiting.

'Well?' she said again.

I tried to sound confident. 'You know how our class is going on that trip to Fota Wildlife Park next week?'

Alice nodded.

'And Miss O'Herlihy said she'd like a parent or two to come along to help supervise?'

This time Alice was smiling as she nodded.

'Why don't you ask your dad to come along?'

Alice hugged me.

'That's brilliant. Dad and Miss O'Herlihy get to spend a whole day together, and I won't even have to get into trouble.'

Now I was starting to get enthusiastic. It wasn't like me.

'And at the end of the day, when they are all friendly, you could tell your dad that you think Miss O'Herlihy fancies him, and you could persuade him to ask her out for coffee or something.'

Alice hugged me again.

'Thanks Meg. That's brilliant. We'll get him to take her out somewhere really nice. I'll tell Mum all about it. She'll get jealous, so she'll dive in and try to save her marriage. Simple.'

I tried to smile. With Alice, nothing was ever simple. But still, maybe I could hope that this plan wouldn't turn out to be a *total* disaster.

* * *

Just before we went home that day, Miss O'Herlihy said,

'Don't forget our trip to Fota is next Tuesday. Has anyone asked their mum or dad if they'd like to come along?'

Chloe put up her hand,

'I asked my mum, Miss.'

I could see Miss O'Herlihy's face go kind of stiff. I knew why. Chloe's mum is always coming in to school causing trouble and giving out about stupid stuff.

'And what did your mum say, Chloe?'

Chloe looked kind of sad.

'She said she'd sooner eat her own leg than go on a bus trip with a gang of rowdy kids.'

Everyone laughed except Chloe. The poor girl didn't even realise that things like that really shouldn't be repeated to teachers.

Just then Alice put up her hand,

'My dad said he'd love to come, Miss,' she said.

Miss O'Herlihy smiled at her.

'That's very nice of him.'

Alice smiled back.

'Well, he loves animals, so he'd be perfect. He could tell us all about them.'

I sighed. Why did Alice always have to get

carried away? As far as I knew, her dad knew nothing at all about animals. In all the time I'd known that family they'd never had as much as a goldfish as a pet. And once, when there was a mouse in their kitchen, Alice's dad jumped up on the table and screamed until Alice chased the mouse outside with the sweeping brush.

Miss O'Herlihy looked around the class.

'Anyone else think their mum or dad would like to come with us?'

I knew for sure that my mum would love to come. It would be her perfect day. She'd bore everyone with talk about endangered animals, and she'd be a total embarrassment. So I put my head down and said nothing.

* * *

Mean Alice waited until I was in her dad's house that evening before surprising him.

She picked her moment when he was engrossed in a documentary on TV.

'Dad?' she said.

He didn't even look up.

'What, love?'

'Do you think you could take a day off work next Tuesday?'

He still didn't look at her.

'Well, I don't really know. Why? Is it for something important?'

Alice nodded.

'Yes, it's something really, really, really important.'

He looked at her for a second.

'What could be all that important?' he asked, before looking back at the TV.

'It's our class trip to Fota Wildlife Park, and I told Miss O'Herlihy you'd come with us.'

Now he looked at her properly.

'Why on earth did you do that?'

Alice put on a really sad face.

'Because now that we're in sixth class, it's our last trip ever. And I missed most of the year because of being in Dublin. And Mum can't come because she's too busy. And it would make it really special for me if you came.'

Now Peter looked kind of sad too.

'Well, maybe I could take the day off,' he said. 'We're not all that busy at the moment. Are there other parents going?'

Alice nodded.

'Oh, lots. Meg's dad is probably going too.'

I made a face at her behind Peter's back. Why did she have to drag my dad into it? My dad would be a bit like Chloe's mum, he'd probably prefer to eat his leg than come with us. Best not to say that to Peter, though. He looked at me.

'Is your dad really going?' he asked.

I could feel my face going red.

'Well, he hopes to,' I mumbled. 'But he's not sure yet. He might have an important meeting.'

Just then the TV documentary got to an exciting bit, with loads of shouting and slamming doors. Alice stood between Peter and the television.

'Well, Dad,' she said. 'Will you come?'

He pushed her aside gently.

'Sure, whatever, just move out of the way for a minute.'

Alice hugged him.

'That's great, Dad. Thanks. You've really made my day.'

I followed Alice as she skipped out of the room. As soon as we were safely in the hall, she gave me a high-five.

'Ha!' she said. 'Step one completed successfully. Dad thinks he's just agreed to a day out. He doesn't know that it's the first step towards a whole new life for our family.'

I couldn't share her excitement. Suddenly everything seemed too complicated again. It was all going to end in tears.

I just knew it.

Then I had a horrible thought.

Imagine if Peter did ask Miss O'Herlihy out?

And imagine if she said yes?

And imagine if they got on really, really well?

And imagine if they fell in love?

How gross would that be?

Would this be the time that Alice finally went too far?

Anyway, there was nothing I could do. The plan had already started, and for once, I couldn't blame Alice.

This time it was already half my fault.

Chapter eight

You couldn't really say that the trip to Fota Island was a total disaster.

It was much worse than that.

First Alice's dad showed up at school in really gross shorts, and a revolting purple and green striped t-shirt. That was bad enough, but even worse was the fact that he wasn't wearing runners and sports socks like a normal person. Instead he was wearing thick, brown sandals with socks under them – green and grey stripy socks like someone's grandad would wear.

After living with my mum for twelve years, I knew plenty about bad dressing, but this was surely beyond a joke.

Peter came over to me.

'Hi, Megan,' he said. 'Where's your dad?'

I could feel my face going red.

'Er, he... I mean... did I tell you he might have an important meeting? Well, he did... so... er... he couldn't come. He wanted to though.'

Peter didn't seem to mind much.

'Oh well,' he said. 'That's his loss. Now I'd better go over to Miss O'H and tell her I'm here.'

As he turned to leave I noticed that there was a huge hole in his left sock, and his big toe was poking out, all hairy and red and curly. Totally, totally gross.

I turned to Alice in horror. I was surprised to see that she seemed quite calm.

'Look at the state of your dad,' I said. 'Aren't

you mad at him?'

Alice sighed.

'Of course I'm mad at him.'

'So what are you going to do about it?'

She sighed again.

'There's nothing I can do, is there? It's too late for him to go home and change, and a big row wouldn't help anything.'

'But how is Miss O'Herlihy going to fall for your dad if he dresses like that?' I asked.

Alice shrugged.

'Lighten up, Megan. It's not his fault. He thinks he's going on a school tour. He doesn't know he's meant to be impressing anyone. And anyway, without Mum to boss him around, he has no idea of how to dress himself properly.'

I wasn't letting her off that easily.

'Well what about you? Have you no control over him? Couldn't you have made him wear something a bit less embarrassing?'

Alice shrugged once again.

'I didn't know, did I? I stayed with Mum last night. I just saw him now, same as you did. That's what this is all about, remember? This whole plan is to get my family back together so fashion disasters like this will never happen again.'

I nodded. I was so shocked at the sight of Peter, I'd kind of forgotten what this was all supposed to be about.

Alice smiled suddenly.

'Anyway, like I said, there's nothing we can do now. Let's hope Miss O'Herlihy can see past the horrible clothes to the nice man inside.'

I glanced over at Miss O'Herlihy who looked quite pretty (for a teacher) in a pale blue dress and sparkly flip-flops. Next to her stood Peter, looking like a very bad joke. I didn't feel like laughing though. This was *so* not a laughing matter.

* * *

As soon as everyone arrived, we all got onto the bus. Miss O'Herlihy sat in the front seat with

Rachel, the class assistant. Alice and I sat on the other front seats, with Grace and Louise just behind us. Melissa and her four buddies grabbed two whole rows of seats. Peter went down to the back seat with all the bold boys. I wondered if maybe it would be best if he jumped out of the emergency door before the bus even got going. Already I had a very bad feeling about the day.

As we drove away from the school, the boys started singing really loudly. Alice nudged me without turning around.

'Just listen to them. Boys can be so immature sometimes.'

I laughed when I heard what they were singing—

'*Oh you have a lovely bottom.........set of teeth.*'

Miss O'Herlihy wasn't very happy though, and she turned around and shouted,

'Really, children, that's hardly appropriate behaviour. You're letting the school down before we even turn the first corner. At your age you should know better. We… '

She suddenly stopped talking, and I turned around to see why. Peter was right in the middle of the group, singing louder than any of the boys. Miss O'Herlihy's face went a sudden pink colour, and she sat back in her seat.

Alice put her head in her hands.

'I can't believe it,' she said. 'He's showing off. He's trying to impress a bunch of bold kids. What have I done?'

* * *

Twenty minutes later, when we were well on the road to Charleville, we came to a huge traffic jam. Cars and lorries were stopped for as far as we could see. Miss O'Herlihy kept looking at her watch.

'We're going to be late. We'll miss our seating for lunch,' she said, 'And then what will we do?'

Just then Peter stood up. Leaving the boys alone in their version of 'You should never push your granny off a bus', he came up to the front of the bus. He tapped the bus-driver on the shoulder.

'I know a short cut,' he said.

The driver scratched his head and said nothing.

'Really,' said Peter, 'We just have to edge forward to this turn here on the left, and then we can bypass Charleville altogether. We'll save loads of time.'

I leaned over and whispered in Alice's ear.

'Didn't you say your dad has a rotten sense of direction? Didn't you tell me he always gets lost when you're on holidays?'

She made a face at me.

'That's different,' she whispered. 'That's on holidays. He knows this road too well to get lost on it. It'll be fine. Dad will get us out of all this traffic, and Miss O'Herlihy will think he's great. This is the best thing that could have happened.'

Still the traffic didn't move, and still the bus driver said nothing.

Peter gave a big long sigh.

'I worked in Cork for years,' he said. 'I know all the back roads.'

Alice grinned at me.

'See?' she said.

The driver looked back at Miss O'Herlihy. Miss O'Herlihy looked at Peter. Peter gave her a charming smile.

'Trust me,' he said.

So Miss O'Herlihy trusted him. She nodded at the driver who edged the bus forwards and took the left turn.

It was a big mistake.

The first thing that worried me was when the driver started to mutter rude words under his breath.

The next thing that worried me was when Peter went back to his seat saying,

'You're the driver, you figure out where we are.'

I could have given Alice a hard time, but I

didn't dare. She was sitting looking out of the window, like none of this had anything to do with her.

I knew things were really bad when the driver pulled into a field and tried to turn the bus around to go back the way we came.

When the bus got stuck in a patch of mud, and we all had to get out and push, it was almost funny.

Only problem was, Miss O'Herlihy didn't seem very amused. She stood under a tree with Rachel, and looked like she'd love to kill some-one. Maybe it was just me, but I had a funny feel-ing that person was Alice's dad.

Alice saw me watching them.

'Don't worry,' she said. 'Everyone's happier when they have a full stomach. Miss O'Herlihy will be fine once she's had her lunch.'

She wished.

Chapter nine

Because of Peter's 'short cut', we were more than an hour late getting to the wildlife park. This made us much too late for our lunch booking in the café. Miss O'Herlihy went in to the café to try to sort something out, and when she came back she didn't look one bit happy.

'They've let another school take our place,' she said. 'Obviously a school that didn't take "short cuts" through fields to get here.'

I thought it was a bit mean of her to say that. After all, Peter had only been trying to help. He didn't deliberately direct the bus driver into a field.

'What are we going to do now, Miss?' I asked.

Miss O'Herlihy sighed.

'The best they can do is let us queue up for our food, and eat it out here on the grass.'

'Yippee!' said Peter. 'A picnic!'

Miss O'Herlihy gave him an evil look.

Peter put his head down.

'Sorry,' he said, 'You looked upset – I was just trying to cheer you up a bit.'

Miss O'Herlihy looked slightly less evil.

'Tell you what,' said Peter. 'You relax out here for a while, and Rachel and I can bring the kiddies in and organise the food. I'll bring you out something nice. How about that?'

Miss O'Herlihy actually smiled at him.

Alice nudged me and said,

'See that, Megan?' she asked. 'I think she likes him.'

'Don't get too carried away,' I said. 'She

doesn't actually like him. She's just noticed his socks, and she feels sorry for him, that's all.'

Everyone except for Miss O'Herlihy went in and queued up for food. Alice and I stayed at the back of the queue where we could keep an eye on Peter and stop him getting into more trouble.

While we were waiting, Rachel walked past with her tray of food.

'Rachel's kind of pretty, isn't she?' said Alice.

I shrugged.

'Mmmm. I suppose. I love her hair. I wish mine was like that.'

'And she's good fun too. She…' began Alice.

Suddenly I realised what was going on. I put my hand up to stop Alice.

'No way,' I said.

Alice looked all innocent.

'But…'

'But what?' I said.

She shrugged.

'OK, I give in. I just thought if things didn't

work out between Dad and Miss O'Herlihy, maybe he could ask Rachel out instead.'

I shook my head.

'No way. This whole thing is *way* too complicated already. Leave Rachel out of it.'

Alice sighed.

'Spoilsport,' she said.

She smiled as she said it though, and I knew she knew that I was right.

Peter got lunch for himself and Miss O'Herlihy, and then squashed two cups of coffee and two large glasses of water onto the tray as well. Alice and I grabbed our food as quickly as we could and followed him outside.

Peter seemed kind of happy, and was humming to himself as he strolled across the grass to where Rachel and Miss O'Herlihy were sitting. Alice started to hum along with him. I had to smile. I leaned over and whispered in her ear.

'What are you going to call Miss O'Herlihy when she's your stepmother?'

She giggled.

'Nothing. 'Cause that's never going to happen. Mum and Dad *can* get back together. They *can* be happy. They just don't know it yet. Once Dad starts dating Miss O'Herlihy, Mum's going to come running back. You just wait and see.'

I felt sure she was wrong, but I didn't argue with her. Alice has always been my best friend, and she deserved my loyalty. All she wanted was her parents to be happy. Was that so bad?

We were near where Miss O'Herlihy and Rachel were sitting when one of the boys shouted,

'Hey, look over there! There's a squirrel under the table.'

The shout must have frightened the poor squirrel, as it bounded out from under the table, and right between Peter's legs.

Peter (who was supposed to love animals so much) gave a funny kind of squeal, and jumped in the air. The tray wobbled, and there was a rattling of dishes. Everything seemed to happen in slow motion. There was a lot more wobbling and rattling, as Peter tried to regain his balance. I suppose he did well not to drop the whole tray, but just as it seemed that disaster had been avoided, one cup of coffee slid off the edge of the tray, right towards Miss O'Herlihy's leg. Peter grabbed for it with one hand, but missed, and the cup fell to the ground, spraying coffee as it went.

Miss O'Herlihy jumped to her feet.

'You've burned my leg,' she screeched.

Quick as a flash, Peter put the tray on the grass, grabbed one of the glasses of water and threw it all over her. It was only one glass of water, but it somehow seemed to soak Miss O'Herlihy from head to foot. It dripped from her hair onto her face, all over her dress and down to her pretty, sparkly flip-flops.

'You big fool,' Miss O'Herlihy shouted.

Peter looked at her surprised.

'But you were burnt,' he said. 'I was trying to save you. Don't you know you should put cold water on burns?'

Miss O'Herlihy looked at him like he was a total eejit.

'I was only splashed. I was fine. And look at me now. I'm like a drowned rat. Am I expected to walk around all day looking like this?'

Just then, Melissa came racing over with a bundle of serviettes.

'Here, Miss,' she said. 'Use these to dry yourself off.'

Miss O'Herlihy smiled at her.

'Why thank you, Melissa,' she said. 'How very thoughtful of you.'

Melissa gave Alice and me an evil smile, and skipped back to her friends. I wished I was the kind of girl who did things like punching their enemies. It was bad enough watching Alice's dad making a complete fool of himself, without having to watch Melissa enjoying it so much.

Eventually we settled down and ate our food. I'd kind of lost my appetite, and by the look of it, so had Miss O'Herlihy. She only picked at the food Peter had chosen for her. When she and Rachel got up to go to the toilet, Peter came and sat by Alice and me.

'Sorry about that,' he said. 'I suppose I embarrassed you a little bit.'

Alice made a face.

'Totally. What are you on, Dad?'

He shrugged.

'Hey, spilling the coffee was an accident. These things happen. Anyway, if it has to be someone's fault, I blame the squirrel.'

Alice rolled her eyes.

'That's big of you, Dad. When you get into trouble, blame the small furry creature.'

I giggled, but stopped quickly when Alice glared at me.

Peter went on.

'And I only threw the water because Miss O'H

said she was burnt. I was trying to save her from more severe burns. How was I supposed to know she was being a drama queen?'

Alice ignored the question.

'And what about the supposed short cut to Charleville?'

'OK. So that was a bit unfortunate. But there used to be a road there, I'm sure of it.'

Alice put on a stern voice.

'And what about the rude songs on the bus?'

He laughed.

'Lighten up, Alice. That was only a bit of a laugh. Even Miss Prissy-Pants should be able to see the funny side in that.'

I sighed. Did Alice still think she could persuade her dad to go out with someone he called a 'drama queen' and 'Miss Prissy Pants'?

Apparently she did. She waggled her finger in Peter's face, and spoke to him like she was the parent and he was the child.

'Look, Dad,' she said. 'I'm warning you. No

more stupid stuff. I want you to behave yourself from now on. OK? Just put your head down and stay out of trouble. You're making a complete show of me and you'll never—'

She stopped suddenly.

'I'll never what?' Peter asked.

'Oh, never mind,' Alice said crossly. 'Just behave, OK?'

Chapter ten

Everyone was tired by the time we got back on the bus for the journey home. Grace and Louise were listening to Grace's new video iPod, so Alice and I got a chance to talk.

'Well?' she said.

'Well what?' I answered, like I didn't know what she was asking.

'How do you think Dad did? Do you think he'd have a chance if he asked Miss O'Herlihy out?'

I probably have a better chance of going out with Johnny Depp. I couldn't say that though. So I said nothing.

Alice continued.

'I don't know what got into him this morning. He was a total klutz – and he's not usually like that. Maybe he was nervous or something. I shouldn't have gone on about how important this day was to me. Still, he was fine after lunch, wasn't he?'

I had to smile.

'You mean except for when he stumbled into the duck-pond?'

Alice made a face.

'Well that duck shouldn't have quacked so loudly. It gave poor Dad a fright.'

'And except for when he was making funny faces at the monkeys, and the zoo-keeper said he should have more sense at his age.'

Now Alice laughed. I was glad to see she still had her sense of humour.

'That doesn't count. Miss O'Herlihy didn't see it, so she can't use that against him.'

I grinned.

'Yeah. Whatever.'

'Anyway,' continued Alice. 'What do you think? Will I tell Dad to ask her out when we get back to the school? Maybe they could go for a cup of coffee on the way home?'

Before I could answer, Peter lurched up along the middle of the bus. He was calling to the bus-driver.

'Can you stop please?'

—The bus-driver ignored him. He was probably still cross over getting lost in the field earlier.

'Stop, please,' repeated Peter. 'It's an emerg—'

Before he could finish the word, he bent over, and threw up loudly and horribly all over the floor of the bus. Everyone around said stuff like 'eeeurgh!' and 'gross!' Everyone except for Melissa who screeched,

'Oh! It's so *totally* disgusting. And some of it

splashed on my new runners.'

That was the best moment of the day.

I turned to Alice.

'You never told me your dad gets car-sick – or should I say bus-sick?'

Alice shook her head. It was hard to understand what she was saying, as she was holding her nose while she spoke. I think she said,

'That's because he doesn't usually get bus-sick. Those bold boys at the back must have fed him too many crisps or something.'

Miss O'Herlihy turned around in horror.

'I can't believe it,' she said. 'I just can't believe it. Why on earth is everything going wrong today?'

I sighed. All I know is, if you want to know why stuff is going wrong, don't ask Alice – she's usually too closely involved to give an honest answer.

The bus pulled in to a lay-by, to give Peter a chance to clean up the mess with the wet-wipes

Miss O'Herlihy practically threw at him. When he'd finished cleaning the floor, he held a clean wipe towards Melissa.

'Would you like me to wipe your shoes for you?' he asked.

Melissa screeched again,

'No way! I am *never* wearing these shoes again. Ever.'

Eventually the bus got going again, and we made it back to school without any more fuss.

Peter was first off the bus, and he vanished before anyone had a chance to talk to him.

I made a face at Alice as we went in to school with some bags of litter.

'Now can you accept that maybe your dad and Miss O'Herlihy are not going to become an item?'

Alice put her head down and didn't answer. She looked so sad, I felt sorry for her.

'Anyway,' I said. 'I suppose I have to take some of the blame. After all, I'm the one who had the idea of your dad going on the trip with us. Maybe a whole day together was a bit too much for them.'

That was the wrong thing to say. Alice suddenly sounded brighter.

'You're right. A whole day *was* too much. We'll have to try again. I bet they could get on fine if they tried. Maybe next week we could...'

We were approaching the bins, and we slowed down when we heard Rachel and Miss O'Herlihy chatting, just around the corner.

Rachel was giggling, and I could hear Miss O'Herlihy's voice.

'Honestly. I've never met anyone like that Peter O'Rourke. He's worse than any child I've ever taught. I have to say I felt sorry when I heard about his wife leaving him. Now that I know him better though, I think she deserves a medal for putting up with him for so long. If I never see that man again, it will be much too soon.'

Alice and I dumped our bags of rubbish, and ran back around the school. Alice put her head in her hands and started to sob.

'Poor Dad,' she sniffled. 'How could she talk about him like that? She made him sound like a total freak.'

Peter had *acted* like a total freak, but I thought it best not to point that out to Alice.

I put my arm around her shoulder.

'Don't cry, Al,' I said. 'Miss O'Herlihy's had a long day, that's all. She's just cross, and tired. We both know your dad's not really like that.'

Alice stopped crying.

'Really?' she asked.

I nodded.

'Really,' I said, and I meant it. 'Your dad's great. He was just unlucky today. Most of that stuff wasn't his fault ... well, not all his fault anyway. And after hearing Miss O'Herlihy saying all those mean things about him, I think he's lucky not to be going out with her. She's not good enough for him if you ask me.'

Alice wiped her eyes.

'Thanks, Meg,' she said.

I smiled at her.

'You're welcome,' I said.

Half the time I don't know what to say to Alice when she's upset, so this time I was very glad I'd been able to find the words to make her feel a bit better.

Alice gave me a small smile.

'Well, at least we know how Miss O'Herlihy feels now. No point wasting any more time trying to get her together with Dad.'

I was so happy I felt like jumping up and down and screaming.

'That's great, Al,' I said. 'I *so* hate all this plotting and scheming. I'm glad it's over at last. Now we can get on with enjoying our last few weeks in sixth class. We can really concentrate on our graduation and we can—'

Alice held up her hand.

'Hey, stop,' she said. 'What are you on about?' she asked.

'You know,' I said. 'That whole thing about getting your dad a girlfriend to make your mum jealous – that was a stupid idea really. So now we can forget all about it.'

Alice suddenly looked cross.

'But that was a *great* idea. It still is. We *have* to get a girlfriend for Dad. That hasn't changed. All that's happened is that Miss O'Herlihy isn't going to be the one – and serves her right too. So we just have to get our act together and find someone else.'

Now I felt like crying.

Why could Alice never, ever, ever give up?

Why had I picked the most stubborn girl in the world to be my best friend?

*   *   *

At school next day, I didn't even smile when Miss O'Herlihy said 'hello' to me. I still felt bad about what she'd said about Alice's dad.

Miss O'Herlihy was extra-nice to Alice though – so nice that at lunchtime Alice said to me – 'Do you think maybe she likes Dad after all?'

I shook my head. How blind could a girl be?

'So why is she being so nice to me?' she asked.

Alice is a bright girl, but this time I was glad she didn't know what was going on. How could I tell her the truth?

Just then Melissa passed by. She stopped walking when she saw us.

'Oh, hi, Alice,' she said. 'I see Miss O'Herlihy is being especially nice to you today. It must be *soooo* embarrassing for you.'

Alice tossed her head.

'I have no idea what you're talking about, Melissa.'

Melissa shrugged.

'Whatever. All I know is, I'd be embarrassed if my teacher was being nice to me just because she felt sorry for me for having such a dorky dad.'

Then she flicked her hair over her shoulders

and walked on.

Alice turned to me. There were tears in her eyes.

'Is that true?' she asked. 'Does Miss O'Herlihy feel sorry for me?'

Of course it was true, but there was no way I was telling Alice. She'd go totally crazy. I shook my head.

'You know what Melissa's like,' I said. 'She's just trying to cause trouble as usual. Let's go find Grace and Louise. Grace has some cool new songs on her iPod.'

I don't know if Alice believed me, but she didn't say any more about it, and neither did I.

I still didn't feel happy though. Alice hadn't given up. Alice *never* gives up.

I knew that even if she didn't talk about it, and even if she seemed to have forgotten all about it, somewhere, deep in her brain, the crazy plan zone would be ticking away quietly. It might take weeks, or even months, but one thing was sure –

sooner or later, Alice would come up with another crazy plan.

I decided it was best to just go on as normal, while I waited for that crazy plan to take shape.

Chapter eleven

When I got home from school one Monday a few weeks later, I found Mum sitting in the middle of the family room floor, surrounded by a huge heap of photographs. It looked like there had been an explosion.

Mum had a funny look on her face, and her eyes were all kind of misty and sparkly.

I ran over to her, worried.

'What's wrong, Mum?' I asked. 'What's happened?'

I was relieved when she smiled.

'Nothing's wrong, love,' she said.

'Then why…?' I pointed to the pile of photographs on the floor. 'What…?'

Mum gazed around her like she'd forgotten that she was sitting in the middle of a photograph mountain.

'Oh, that,' she said. 'Don't worry about that. I'm just happy.'

What kind of a crazy mother was I stuck with?

Why couldn't she dance around when she was happy, like normal people do?

I picked up a photograph from the pile and glanced at it, wondering who those sad losers in the dodgy clothes could be. Then I looked again, as I slowly realised what I was looking at. I gulped hard, and looked one more time.

It was a picture of Mum and Dad that must surely have been taken as a joke. Mum's hair is almost down to her waist, in a big cascade of dull, brown frizz. She has so much hair it's a wonder she's able to hold her head up straight. She's wearing a huge, floaty, yellow dress that comes down to her ankles, making her look like an overgrown daffodil. Dad's hair is long too, and greasy too by the look of it – it's hanging down around his shoulders like lots of rats' tails. Even worse, though, Dad's actually wearing dungarees – big, baggy, denim dungarees – and he doesn't even look embarrassed. He's actually smiling and waving at the camera like he's proud of himself. I made up my mind to slag him over the photo – if I ever got over the shock, that is.

Mum took the photo from my hand and gazed at it. She spoke dreamily.

'Your dad and I were so happy then.'

I giggled.

'Why? Was it because you were on your way to a fancy dress party, and you knew you had the funniest outfits?'

'Ha, ha. Very amusing,' she said.

I picked up some more photographs. They all seemed to be taken at around the same time, at some kind of a concert or festival. I couldn't look at them for long. They were making me dizzy with their bright colours.

'When was this?' I asked.

Mum sighed a big, long, happy sigh.

'At the Foggy Mountain music festival – in Galway. Dad and I went there just after we got married. It was the best weekend of my whole life. And you'll never guess what …'

'What? You got arrested by the fashion police?'

She ignored my joke. (A pity, 'cause I thought it was quite funny.)

'I just heard on the radio that there's going to be a Foggy Mountain reunion at the weekend. It's so lucky I heard it. Imagine if I'd missed it!'

'Sorry, Mum,' I said. 'I couldn't imagine anything as terrible as you not finding out about the

Foggy Mountain reunion.'

Mum kept talking.

'It's going to be in the same place, and they've got some of the same bands coming to play. We're going to go for the weekend. It's time I let my hair down.'

I put my hands over my face and screamed in mock fear.

'Not that. Anything but that. Promise me you won't let your hair down.'

Mum just kept talking like I hadn't said a word – very strange. By now I should be getting her lecture on 'showing respect for adults.'

'We're going to camp in the same field where we camped twenty years ago,' Mum said. 'It's going to be a real trip down memory lane.'

'You'd better be careful,' I said. 'Memory Lane sounds like it's full of mad old hippies. It could be a real scary place.'

Once again Mum ignored my joke. She looked at the first photograph again.

'I must look up in the attic. I think I might have that dress still.'

I laughed.

'Why? Are you going to use it as a tent? You'd be very popular – you could fit a few families in there.'

Mum must really have been in a strange mood, because she ignored that joke too. Suddenly I had a horrible thought – probably the scariest thought of my whole life.

Did Mum expect me to go hang out with all these crazy people with psychedelic clothes and horror hair?

Did she think I was going to spend my whole weekend dancing around a mucky field listening to creepy old music?

Knowing my luck I'd probably get my picture in the paper, and that would give Melissa enough to mock me about all the way to the summer holidays.

Did Mum want to ruin my life forever?

I was so scared I could hardly get the words out.

'I... I... I... don't have to go, do I?'

Mum shook her head.

'No, love. I'm sorry. I'd love you to come, but it's not really suitable for kids. You and Rosie will stay here. It's all arranged. Linda's coming to mind you.'

Now that was *really* good news. Linda is Mum's younger sister. We hardly ever see her because she lives in Dublin, and has a very busy life. When she visits though, she's really fun, and always gives Rosie and me sweets when Mum isn't looking. A whole weekend with her would be totally *brilliant*.

Mum suddenly looked sad.

'I hope we're doing the right thing,' she said. 'Dad and I have never spent a night away from Rosie before. And she's still only a baby. Maybe it's best if you and Rosie just come with us. Maybe I should ring Linda and tell her not to come after all.'

There was *no way* I was going on that crazy trip. I jumped up.

'No, Mum,' I said. 'Don't do that. Rosie's not a baby. She's four now. She's a big girl. And I'll help to mind her. And I'll be really good for Linda. I'll help her all the time. I'll—'

Mum laughed.

'OK. OK. I get the message. I suppose you can stay here. It will be good for you girls to spend some time with Linda – get to know her a bit better. Now would you ever get the ladder from the garage for me? I'm going up to the attic to see if I can find that lovely yellow dress.'

Chapter twelve

The List
No more than 1 hour
of TV a day
No Sweets
No Crisps

Twenty minutes later, Mum was up in the attic humming ancient songs as she rummaged through boxes of old junk. Before long, she called me,

'Come, on up, Megan. You can help me. This is so much fun.'

I thought doing really hard maths homework would be more fun than helping Mum, but I decided not to say this.

'Sorry, Mum,' I called. 'I'd love to, but I promised Alice I'd call for her.'

Mum didn't even answer, so I took the

opportunity to escape.

I ran over to Alice's place. Alice laughed when I told her the good news that Mum and Dad were going away.

'You lucky thing,' she said. 'A whole weekend without your mum and dad bossing you around. I'm jealous already.'

Then she thought for a minute.

'Who's going to mind you though? Who does your mother trust to fill you up with organic porridge, and to keep you away from evil things like television and mobile phones?'

I laughed.

'That's the really great news. My Aunt Linda is coming to mind us. She's really cool – well, I suppose not really, *really* cool, but she's a lot cooler than Mum, that's for sure. She'll promise Mum loads of stuff, but as soon as we're on our own, she'll act like a normal person. It's going to be so—'

Alice put up a hand to stop me. She had that

funny look on her face again.

'I think I remember your Aunt Linda from when she visited before.'

I nodded.

'Yeah. She comes down about once a year. She never stays long though. After a day or two she starts to get restless and wants to go home. She—'

Alice stopped me again.

'She's kind of pretty, isn't she?'

Linda's my aunt. I'd never really thought about whether she was pretty before.

'I don't really know,' I said. 'She doesn't look much like my mum, and that's a good thing, I suppose. She has nice, shiny, black, curly hair. And she wears cool clothes. Well, cool for an aunt anyway.'

Why was Alice grinning so much?

And why was she suddenly so interested in my Aunt Linda?

By now Alice was looking like she'd just won

the lottery.

'Linda never got married, did she?' she asked.

Suddenly everything became clear.

'No way!' I said. 'No *way* are you going to involve my aunt in one of your crazy plans.'

Alice ignored me.

'She's not married though, is she?'

I shook my head.

'Not last time I asked.'

'And does she have a boyfriend?'

I was fairly certain that Linda didn't have a boyfriend. I'd heard Mum and Dad talking about that very subject just a few weeks earlier. This was crazy though. Alice was getting carried away as usual.

Alice shook my shoulder.

'Come on, Meg. Tell me. Does Linda have a boyfriend?'

'Not that I know of,' I said quietly.

Alice gave a big happy shout.

'That's settled then. We'll arrange a little

romance between Dad and Linda, make sure Mum gets to hear of it, and before we know it, Mum will be begging Dad to let her move back in. Simple.'

I walked away from her and looked out the window. Alice's old swings were swaying in the breeze. We used to spend hours on those swings, chatting about stupid things. I thought about how easy things were when her parents were together, and all Alice and I had to do all day long was hang out, and do fun stuff.

At Easter, when Alice and her mum moved back to Limerick, I thought everything was going to be OK again.

Suddenly I felt really selfish – I had got what I wanted. My best friend was back, and I never really stopped to think that she was still upset that her parents didn't live together any more. I thought that since they lived near to each other, everything was fine. How totally stupid was that?

Alice came over and stood next to me. She spoke quietly.

'Linda will only be here for a few days. It's a perfect opportunity, and we can't let it pass us by. Please help me, Meg. Just this one more time.'

I put my head down. As far as I could see I had two choices – I could agree to help Alice right now, or I could let her spend the next week persuading me, and then agree. Whatever happened, I knew I'd end up in the middle of another crazy Alice plan, sooner or later.

Suddenly I felt tired of it all. I was in sixth class. This was supposed to be a fun year, the best year of primary school, maybe the best of my whole life – and I'd already spent half of it running around helping Alice with stupid plans that never worked properly anyway.

Alice left my side and went to sit on her bed. After a minute, I turned around to look at her. Her face was so sad, it made me want to cry. What kind of a friend was I if I only liked her when she was happy?

I went and stood beside her.

'No crazy stuff this time, OK?'

She jumped up and hugged me.

'I promise,' she said. 'No crazy stuff at all. It'll be a crazy-free zone. Thanks, Meg. You're the best friend I could ever have.'

I tried to smile, but I couldn't.

*   *   *

The rest of that week was very strange. Mum kept arriving down from the attic carrying bundles of revolting brightly-coloured clothes. She'd toss them onto the kitchen table with big happy sighs.

'Aaaaah,' she'd say. 'Everything was so simple and bright and happy in those days.'

Mostly I ignored her, or sometimes when it got too much I pretended to vomit. Mum never seemed to mind. It was as if she'd already vanished from us and gone back to her past, where I didn't even exist yet.

One day, when Dad got home from work Mum waved a big heap of denim in front of his face. He took it from her, and held it up. I giggled. It was the old denim dungarees he'd had on in the photograph.

'Look, Donal,' Mum said. 'Remember these? You can wear them to the festival at the weekend.'

Dad went pale.

'I don't think so, Sheila. They're ... well, they're ancient history aren't they? I like to think I've moved on a bit since then.'

Mum hugged him.

'Go on. Try them on, please, for me.'

Dad looked very uncomfortable as he went out in to the hall. Seconds later he shuffled back into the room. Even Mum had to laugh. Dad looked so pathetic it was hard to believe. He looked like someone in a very, very bad fancy dress outfit. Rosie even looked a bit scared. She went over and half-hid behind Mum's legs.

'Daddy's a loser,' she said.

Dad made a face at Mum.

'Happy?' he said. 'Even my own daughter thinks I look ridiculous.'

Mum put her hand over her mouth and tried to stop laughing.

'OK, so maybe you shouldn't wear these. I'll look in the attic for something else.'

Dad shook his head.

'Actually, Sheila, you won't. I'm wearing my normal jeans or I'm not going. OK?'

Mum was quiet for a minute, and then she nodded.

'I suppose so. Now I wonder if I can find your old sandals?'

'*Sheila.*'

Now Dad sounded really cross.

Mum backed down.

'OK, no more old stuff I promise. Now get changed again. The lentil stew is almost ready.'

After dinner Mum put away all the crazy

clothes, and went back to work on *'The List'*.

This was her list of instructions for Linda. All stupid stuff like:

No more than one hour of TV per day for the girls

No processed foods

No sweets

No crisps

Dad leaned over her shoulder and started to read.

'Linda's your sister.' he said. 'Don't you trust her to mind the girls properly?'

Mum looked all stressed.

'I do trust her – sort of. I'd just like to think that she's doing things my way, that's all.'

Dad went back to his paper.

'Whatever,' he said.

I smiled to myself. Poor Mum. Linda had only minded Rosie and me once before, for an afternoon, and in that time she managed to break almost every one of Mum's stupid rules. Mum could write all the lists she liked, I knew Linda would ignore every single word. We were going to have so much fun – I knew it already.

Now all I had to worry about was Alice and her crazy plan.

Chapter thirteen

Linda arrived on Friday afternoon. She was a bit late, so Mum and Dad had to leave almost immediately. Mum stood in the hall and hugged Rosie and me like hugs were going out of fashion.

'Oh my precious little babies,' she said, 'I am going to miss you so, so much.'

Dad grinned at me over Mum's shoulder.

'If we don't get moving, Sheila,' he said, 'It'll be too late to pitch the tent and we'll have to book in to a hotel.'

Mum let go of Rosie and me like we were on fire.

'No way. No hotels for us. We're camping, just like we did the last time.'

She backed out the door.

'Bye girls. Love you both. Be good. Bye Linda. I left a list of instructions on the kitchen table. I'll phone you tomorrow to see how you're getting on. Bye girls. Love you lots. Do what Linda tells you. Don't forget…'

By now Mum was in the car and Dad was driving away. Soon they were out of sight, and if Mum was still giving instructions, it didn't matter because we couldn't hear them anymore.

Linda took Rosie by the hand and the three of us went into the kitchen. Linda picked up 'The List' and read it carefully. Then she stuck it onto the fridge, with the writing turned in.

'I'm in charge now,' she said.

She reached into her handbag,

'Anyone feel like a Mars Bar?'

Rosie and I ran and grabbed the chocolate. This was going to be so, so good. This was going to be like Christmas – only better.

Pity there was just one small problem.

A few minutes later, the problem rang the doorbell.

I let Alice in and brought her in to the kitchen. Linda gave her a bar of chocolate too. I wondered if she'd have been quite so nice if she'd known exactly what Alice had planned for her.

While Linda played with Rosie, Alice and I went to my room.

Alice threw herself on to my bed.

'I've learned a lot from the thing with Miss O'Herlihy,' she said.

'Like what?' I said. 'Like not meddling in your father's love life?'

She shook her head.

'No. Not that actually. This time we're going to take things more slowly. We'll let Dad and Linda meet tonight, just for a minute, just long enough for them to kind of wonder about each other, and then tomorrow we'll get down to the serious stuff.'

I sighed.

'So how are we going to get them to meet tonight?'

'Duh. That's easy. I just stay here until Dad calls me for tea.'

'But he won't come over here. He'll phone you, like he always does.'

Alice smiled.

'He can phone, but it won't do him a whole lot of good.'

I didn't bother asking what she meant by that – I knew I'd find out sooner or later.

After about twenty minutes, Alice's phone rang. It played a really cool tune, and a whole row of lights began flashing up and down the side of the phone. For about the millionth time I wished that Mum and Dad would escape from the Dark Ages and let me have a phone.

Alice grinned at me, and picked up her phone.

'It's Dad. I'll put him on speaker,' she said, as she pressed a button.

'Hello?' she said.

'Alice, it's time for you to come home for tea.'

Peter's voice was as clear as if he was standing next to us.

'Hello?' said Alice again, slightly louder this time.

Peter's reply was louder too.

'It's Dad. I said it's time to come home for tea.'

'Hello?' said Alice for the third time. 'Who is this? You'll have to speak up.'

'I said – Come. Home. For. Tea.' This time it sounded as if Peter was standing right next to me and shouting in my ear.

Alice grinned at me.

'I'm sorry, whoever you are,' she said. 'You keep breaking up on me. Why don't you try calling back later?'

'Alice, if you don't—' began her dad, but Alice

clicked off her phone.

'Oops,' she said. 'He seems to have got cut off.'

Then she gave a big fake sigh.

'Mobile phones these days. They're so unreliable.'

I had to laugh, but I was thinking that I would never, ever be brave enough to do what Alice had just done. (Anyway, if Mum has her way, I'll never get the chance, as I won't ever have a phone.)

Three minutes later, Alice's little brother Jamie was at the front door.

'Dad says come home for tea,' he said. 'And if you ever again do that stupid trick of pretending not to hear him on the phone, he's going to take it from you and keep it for six months.'

I giggled until Alice made me stop by glaring at me.

I was glad her dad hadn't called over to pick her up, but not for long.

'Don't worry,' Alice whispered as she left. 'I have a plan B. See you after tea, and I'll tell you all about it.'

Half an hour later she was back. She dragged me into the garage, and opened the fuse box.

'Lucky this is the same as the one in my house,' she said. 'That makes things a bit easier.'

I was starting to feel scared.

'What exactly are you doing? I don't think Mum and Dad will be too happy if you blow up the house.'

She made a face at me.

'I'm not totally stupid you know.'

Then she reached up and flicked a switch marked *Lights*.

'All I've done is switch off the lights. Will Linda know how to fix them do you think?'

I shook my head.

'Linda is totally useless at stuff like that. Mum always teases her that she has to call an electrician to change a plug.'

Alice gave a happy smile.

'That's what I hoped. So later on, when it gets dark, Dad will have to come and save the day. Linda will be so impressed that she'll be dying to see him again tomorrow.'

I wasn't so sure about that, but as Alice's plans go, this one seemed harmless enough, so I said nothing and we went back into the house to wait for it to get dark.

Some time later, Linda, Rosie, Alice and I were lying on the floor in the family room watching our second hour of television. I was full from the yummy Chinese takeaway we'd had for tea, and the three bags of crisps and the litre bottle of lemonade that we'd finished between us.

Alice nudged me. I repeated the line she'd made me practise earlier.

'It's getting a bit dark, isn't it?'

Linda ignored me. She was busy feeding Rosie even more crisps.

Five minutes later, Alice tried.

'It's getting a bit dark. Will I put the light on, Linda?'

This time Linda paid attention.

'Sure. Thanks, Alice.'

Alice got up and made a big production of flicking the switch.

'Doesn't seem to be working,' she said.

Now Linda sat up.

'Probably just the bulb.'

Alice ran into the kitchen and loudly flicked the lights.

'No, they're all broken.'

Now Linda stood up.

'Oh well,' she said. 'It's too late to get the lights fixed tonight. It'll be fun sitting here by candle-light. Where does your mum keep the candles, Megan?'

Alice poked me hard in the ribs.

'Er, em, we don't have any candles,' I said. 'Mum em... she...'

Alice dived in.

'Megan's mum thinks candles are a fire hazard. She doesn't allow them in the house.'

Linda made a face.

'That *does* sound like Sheila. But what will we do, Megan? I don't fancy a whole night in the dark. Do you know the name of your electrician? Do you think he'd come out at night?'

Alice grinned at her.

'You don't need an electrician. I'll get my dad. He's brilliant at stuff like this.'

'Are you sure?' asked Linda. 'I wouldn't like to bother him.'

Alice nodded.

'Sure I'm sure. He's very kind-hearted. He'd love to help.'

Minutes later Peter was at the door. It took him about three seconds to figure out that the fuse switch had tripped. He flicked it back, and the house lit up instantly. Linda clapped her hands like Peter had just performed a magic trick.

Peter looked puzzled.

'That really shouldn't happen,' he said. 'But call me if the lights go out again.'

Linda smiled at him.

'Thank you so, so much. I don't know what we'd have done without you.'

Peter smiled back at her.

'Don't mention it,' he said.

Then he went back home, whistling as he went.

'What a nice, helpful man,' Linda said as she closed the front door.

Alice smiled as she whispered in my ear.

'Did you hear that? She said he was nice. And did you hear Dad whistling? He only whistles when he's really happy. I think they like each other. We're halfway there. I'm looking forward to tomorrow already.'

I wanted to know what she had planned, but at the same time, I didn't want to know. It didn't matter anyway, as it didn't look like she was going to tell me.

Alice went towards the door.

'Time I went home,' she said. 'Get a good night's sleep, Meg. You're going to need it. Tomorrow is going to be a very busy day.'

Chapter fourteen

Next morning Alice arrived early. She came into my bedroom and kind of fizzed around the place, picking things up and putting them down in the wrong places – stuff like that. I'd made up my mind to be tough, so as soon as she sat down I said the words I'd been practising in my head.

'Tell me your plan or I won't help you.'

Alice laughed.

'OK. OK.'

I was surprised.

'You mean just like that? You're not even going to argue with me?'

Alice shrugged.

'Argue? Me?'

I had to laugh at her as she continued.

'It's no biggie anyway. We're just going to plan a romantic dinner date for Dad and Linda. It'll be perfect. It'll—'

I interrupted her.

'How exactly are you going to set that up? Are you going to get into their minds? Are you going to magically persuade Peter to ask Linda out? Are you going to magically persuade her to accept? Maybe it's just me, but I don't think you're going to pull this off.'

Alice made a pouty face.

'Of course I'll pull this off. Have I ever failed before?'

Hello?

Had Alice's memory just evaporated?

What about the disaster with Miss O'Herlihy?

What about mid-term when she tried to get rid of her mum's boyfriend who turned out not to be a boyfriend anyway?

What about the time Alice hid under my bed for days on end?

It didn't seem fair to remind her of all this stuff, so I just avoided the issue.

'Anyway,' I said, 'Linda can't go out on a romantic dinner date. She might ignore most of Mum's rules and regulations, but she won't go out and leave Rosie and me here on our own. Mum would surely hear about it, and she'd never forgive her. Ever.'

Alice grinned.

'Don't worry. I've thought of that. I've thought of everything. The romantic date is going to be here.'

'But how… ?'

Alice waved her hand in the air.

'I'll tell you later. For now, all we have to do is

convince Linda that you and I should cook dinner tonight.'

As she spoke, she set off into the kitchen, dragging me behind her. Linda was busy pouring brightly-coloured cereal into a bowl for Rosie. Rosie was smiling so much it looked like her face was going to burst.

'Look, Megan,' she said, 'Linda's nice. No yucky porridge.'

Linda made a face at me.

'I won't tell your mum if you don't.'

I laughed.

'It can be our little secret.'

Alice nudged me, so I continued.

'Er…Linda?'

Linda looked up.

'Yes?'

'How about if Alice and I cook dinner tonight?'

Linda shrugged.

'Why would you want to do that?'

Alice piped up.

'It's a project we have to do ….. for Guides.'

Linda looked surprised.

'I didn't know you went to Guides, Megan,' she said.

(Maybe that's because I don't.)

I smiled and tried to think of an answer that wasn't the truth, but wasn't a lie either.

'Well, Mum thinks Guides are good. She thinks Guides do lots of helpful environmental stuff.'

This was kind of true. I'd never exactly heard Mum say that, but I bet it's what she thinks.

Linda smiled.

'Well, I don't see why you can't cook dinner. Otherwise we would have been ordering another takeaway.'

I felt like crying. I *love* takeaway food, and Mum *never* lets us get it. Did Alice have any idea what I was giving up for her?

Linda continued,

'What are you going to cook?'

I looked desperately at Alice who was playing with Rosie and didn't see me.

'Er… em… it's a surprise,' I muttered.

Linda laughed.

'Good. I just love surprises.'

I smiled weakly. After tonight Linda might not love surprises quite so much.

Then Alice grabbed me by the arm and dragged me next door to her house. I was starting to worry that by the end of the weekend, one of my arms was going to be a few centimetres longer than the other.

Peter was in the family room watching TV.

Alice went and sat on the edge of his chair.

'Great news, Dad,' she said. 'Linda has invited you to dinner.'

Peter looked up at her.

'Linda who?'

Alice poked him in the shoulder.

'You know – Linda, Megan's aunt. She'd like

you to come to dinner in their house tonight.'

Now Peter looked puzzled.

'Why would she want that?'

It was time for my line.

'She just wants to thank you for helping her with the lights last night.'

Peter laughed.

'I only flicked a switch. That hardly deserves a dinner invitation.'

'Well,' said Alice. 'Linda's very… she's very… what is she Megan?'

'Er, she's … very… she's very spontaneous.'

Peter still didn't look convinced.

'Who else is going?'

'Well, Megan, and me and Rosie,' said Alice.

Peter shook his head.

'I don't know really. I…'

Alice smiled at him.

'I thought you'd be glad not to be eating pizza again, so I've already said you'll go. Eight o'clock. OK?'

Peter put his hands up in surrender.

'OK. OK. I give up. A nice dinner would be a pleasant change. I'll be there. Now be quiet and let me watch this match.'

* * *

Half an hour later Alice and I were on the way to the shop with the money Linda had given us.

'What are we going to cook?' I asked. 'I only know how to make stew, and that's not very romantic, is it?'

Alice shook her head.

'No way. No stew.'

'What about those noodle things you ate when you were hiding in my room?' I suggested. 'We'd only have to boil the kettle and they'd be ready.'

Alice shook her head even more quickly.

'Absolutely no way. Those noodles were totally gross.'

I was getting a bit fed up.

'What do *you* suggest then?' I asked. 'Since you're so clever.'

Alice stopped walking and looked at me.

'There's loads of lettuce in your garden isn't there?'

I nodded.

'Our garden has more lettuce than grass.'

'OK. So, salad to start, then lasagne for main course – we can buy it ready made, so no cooking. And then ice cream for dessert. And if we've enough money left, a nice bottle of champagne to finish it all off. Easy-peasy.'

I still wasn't happy.

'OK,' I said. 'So the food is sorted, but we still have one very big problem. What's Linda going to say when Peter shows up for dinner, and she hasn't even invited him?'

Alice grinned at me.

'Nothing,' she said.

I was sorry I was too mature to stamp my foot.

'What do you mean "nothing"? Do you think Linda is going to somehow forget that she hasn't invited him?'

Alice laughed.

'Of course not. She'll know perfectly well that she hasn't invited him. But she's an adult. She's got to be polite. Can you really imagine her saying – "What are you doing here? – Go home – You're not invited"?'

I giggled.

'I can't see Linda saying that.'

'Well then, we're sorted. Aren't we? Later she can ask you what's going on, but she can't say anything to Dad tonight – not while he's still here. She'll just have to play along. And we only need this to work for one night. Mum will find out that Dad was here on a romantic date, and then everything will change.'

'But what if your mum doesn't find out?'

Even as I said the words, I knew the answer. Alice was going to make very sure that her mum found out – after all, that was the whole idea, and Alice wasn't going to leave anything to chance.

I didn't argue any more. There wasn't any

point. But by now I'd had far too much experience of Alice's clever plans. I was fairly sure that this plan was going to end up like all of the others – a total mess.

I decided I'd just better stick around to make sure that no one got killed.

Chapter fifteen

The girl at the checkout in the supermarket was very nice, but no matter how much Alice begged her, she wouldn't let us buy a bottle of champagne.

'Sorry, girls,' she said. 'I didn't come down in the last shower of rain, so don't even try to pretend that you're eighteen.'

Alice and I spoke together.

'It's for my dad.'

'It's for my aunt.'

The girl laughed.

'Here's a little bit of advice girls – next time, at least try to get your stories straight.'

Alice protested.

'But it is for my dad and her aunt. It's for both of them. They're ... well... what I mean is...'

The girl took the champagne from the conveyer belt, and stood it on a shelf behind her.

'Whatever. I don't care if it's for your granny and her pet elephant, just tell them if they want it, they'll have to come here and get it for themselves. OK?'

Even Alice didn't dare to argue any more, so we just paid for the rest of the shopping and left the supermarket.

We got back to my place and stashed all the food in the fridge. Then Alice took me next door to her house. She wouldn't tell me why, of course, so I just followed her and waited to see what would happen.

Alice rooted around in all the kitchen cupboards for ages, and at last she pulled out a bottle of champagne.

'Ha!' she said. 'I knew that was in there somewhere.'

'Are you going to just take it?' I asked.

She nodded.

'Sure. We can't buy any, and I think a romantic date needs champagne, don't you?'

I sighed. I'm only twelve, what am I meant to know about romantic dates?

I tried again.

'Surely your dad will notice the champagne is missing from his cupboard?'

She shook her head.

'Nah. It's been there for years. Actually I think Dad gave it to Mum for her birthday a couple of years ago.'

'Great,' I said. 'On your dad's hot date he's going to be drinking his wife's bottle of champagne. Very romantic, I'm sure.'

Alice put down the bottle and glared at me.

'You're right. It's not really all that romantic, but this is an emergency.'

'OK. OK,' I said. 'As long as you're sure your dad won't recognise it.'

Alice laughed.

'Don't worry. Dad knows zero about champagne. He'll have no idea, I promise. Now, you go and distract Linda, and I'll hide this. Where would you think would be a good place?'

I laughed.

'How about in the fridge, under the huge bag of organic spinach? Linda definitely won't look there.'

*   *   *

Later, when the champagne was safely hidden away, Linda took Alice, Rosie and me into town. She bought us all hot chocolate with extra marshmallows, and Rosie was so happy she couldn't talk for about ten minutes. She just sat there sipping her drink and smiling like crazy.

Then we went into Threads and Linda let us each pick out a t-shirt. We pretended to say 'no thanks' at first, but luckily Linda insisted.

'I got a pay-rise last week,' she said. 'And I have to spend it on something.'

I sighed. I love my mum, but I wished she could be a bit more like her sister.

*　　*　　*

When we got home, I wanted to start getting the dinner ready. Alice wouldn't let me though.

'Jamie's staying with Mum tonight,' she said. 'And I promised Dad I'd walk him over to her place.'

Hmmm. How convenient, I thought.

We collected Jamie from his dad's house and took him around the corner to Veronica's apartment. She asked us in, and I had no choice but to follow Alice inside.

Alice didn't waste any time. Before I'd even sat down, she said,

'Guess what, Mum? Dad has a date tonight.'

In films, when that kind of thing happens, the mum puts her head in her hands and sobs dramatically, saying stuff like – *'How could he do this to me?'* and *'But doesn't he understand? I love him – I'll always love him.'*

It looked like Veronica doesn't watch the right films though. She actually laughed.

'Your dad? A date? I don't think so, Alice.'

Alice got cross.

'Why wouldn't he have a date? He's a very good-looking man. My teacher even said so.'

I made a face at her. Our teacher had said a lot of stuff about Peter, but I'd never heard her say that he was good-looking.

Veronica didn't seem to wonder why Miss O'Herlihy would be saying anything at all about Peter.

'Well, maybe your dad is good-looking – in his own way,' she said. 'But a date? He's not really the type, is he?'

Alice stamped her foot.

'Well, maybe you don't know him very well. He *has* a date. It's with Megan's aunt. They're having a romantic dinner tonight. He's really looking forward to it. In fact, he talked about nothing else all morning.'

Veronica smiled.

'Well, good luck to him,' she said. 'I hope he has a very nice time. Now, would any of you like something to drink?'

Alice answered for me.

'No. We're fine. We have to go and… well, we just have to go. See you tomorrow.'

When we were outside, I wasn't sure what I felt. It didn't sound like Veronica was very jealous, and if she wasn't jealous, the whole plan was a waste of time before it even started.

Maybe I could stop this before it went any further. I tried to sound casual.

'Your mum didn't seem very jealous, did she?'

Alice shrugged.

'Well, she wouldn't would she? She can't let on.

She has to act cool in front of us. Inside I bet she's really upset. She'll think about Dad's hot date all night, and tomorrow, when she hears what a success it was, she'll go crazy – I know it. She'll—'

I interrupted her.

'But what if tonight's date isn't a success, what then?'

Alice marched on ahead.

'We don't have to worry about that. Tonight *will* be a success. I've decided. Now let's get going. We've got a lot to do.'

Chapter sixteen

Next Alice insisted that we go back to her dad's house. I was starting to feel dizzy from being in so many places.

'Can't we just go to my house?' I suggested.

'We will,' said Alice. 'In a minute. I need to get some stuff first.'

'What stuff?' I asked.

But by now Alice was halfway up the stairs to her bedroom.

'Just stuff,' she said. 'You'll see.'

When we got to her room, Alice took out her hair-straightener, and a big bag of clips and hair slides. Then she opened all her drawers and pulled out every piece of make-up she'd ever owned, and spread it all out on her bed.

She gave a big sigh.

'I haven't got all that much. Don't suppose you have anything stashed away?'

I shook my head.

'No chance. You know what Mum's like. She *"doesn't approve of make-up for twelve-year-olds."*'

Alice giggled, '*Or* for — what is she now — thirty-seven-year-olds?'

I had to laugh too. I don't think my mum has ever even touched a lipstick, let alone owned one.

Then I stopped laughing.

'Hey,' I said. 'What's all this for anyway? Why

are you suddenly so interested in wearing make-up? And it's not like we're going out anywhere – you're spending the evening in my kitchen, remember?'

Alice shook her head.

'The make-up's not for me, Dork-head. I'm not the one going on a romantic date, am I?'

I laughed again as I picked up a sparkly eye shadow.

'Hmmm,' I said. 'I think this shade would be perfect on your dad. Just right to bring out the blue in his eyes.'

'Ha, ha,' said Alice. 'Very funny. Not. You know well that all this stuff is for Linda.'

I sighed.

'Well, I suppose I know now,' I said. 'But Linda doesn't need all that make-up. She's pretty enough as she is.'

Alice started to gather up the stuff and put it into a giant make-up bag.

'Careful, Meg,' she said. 'Don't start sounding

like your mother. Never forget, there's no one so pretty she can't be improved with some nice make-up.'

'Now who's sounding like her mother?' I snapped.

Alice gave me a quick hug.

'Sorry,' she said. 'I shouldn't have said that. Let's just agree that neither of us is going to turn into our mothers. Ever. OK?'

I nodded. I didn't want to fight with Alice. And besides, messing about with make-up would be fun – especially without Mum there looking over my shoulder and saying I was wasting my life.

There was still one problem thought.

'What are we going to say to Linda?' I asked. 'We can't say – "Hey, Linda, you'd better put on some make-up, just in case a handsome prince happens to drop by tonight?"'

Alice suddenly started to laugh so much she couldn't talk. When she finally recovered, she said,

'I don't think you could exactly call my dad a handsome prince. Do you?'

Now I laughed too.

'Maybe if we got him to wear a satin shirt ......'

'...... and some white tights,' added Alice.

'...... and we could borrow a donkey from the donkey sanctuary and he could arrive on that ....' I finished.

By now we were both laughing so much we had to lie on the bed and roll around for a while. It was nice.

Eventually Alice sat up.

'Enough of that,' she said. 'Let's go next door. We've got work to do.'

* * *

Linda was surprised when Alice and I suggested that we give her a makeover. She even sounded a little bit insulted.

'Actually I'm quite happy with the way I look,' she said.

Alice smiled her best smile.

'You look fab,' she said. 'But we have to give someone a makeover, and there's no-one else around.'

Linda looked a bit less cross.

'But why do you have to give someone a make-over?' she asked.

I looked desperately at Alice.

'It's a project,' she said.

'For Guides,' I added. That sounded a bit stupid, but by the time I realised that, the words were already out of my mouth.

'Hmmmm,' said Linda. 'Guides must have changed a lot since I was there. In my day it was mostly about lighting camp-fires and tying complicated knots and polishing shoes for old ladies.'

'Oh, Guides is very different nowadays,' said Alice. 'We do all kinds of interesting stuff. Last week we went white-water rafting.'

I kicked Alice to quieten her. Did that girl *never* know when to stop?

Linda looked like she didn't believe Alice, but

she didn't say so.

'Well,' she said. 'If you're going to do my make-up I suppose we'd better get on with it. I'm getting even older and wrinklier while we're standing here talking about it.'

Alice did most of the work. I didn't mind, because I didn't have much of an idea what to do anyway. Mostly I just held brushes, and ran and got damp cotton wool whenever something went wrong. (Which seemed to happen an awful lot.)

After a while, Rosie came in from the garden. She'd never seen anyone putting on make-up before, so she just sat quietly, and watched with her mouth open.

After ages Alice was finished the make-up.

Linda was impatient.

'Can I see?' she asked.

'We're not finished yet,' said Alice. 'What about straightening your hair?'

Linda shook her head.

'Thanks, but no thanks,' she said. 'I actually like my curls, and I'm not having them straightened. Not even for the sake of your Guide project.'

'But…' began Alice.

I interrupted her.

'Forget it, Al,' I said. 'Leave Linda's hair alone. It's really lovely already.'

'OK. OK,' muttered Alice. 'I was only trying to help. I suppose you're ready so.'

She stood back and admired Linda's face.

'What do you think?' she said to me.

I didn't really know what to think. Linda looked different, but I'm not sure she looked better. She just didn't look like herself any more.

Alice handed Linda a mirror. She looked at herself for ages, but she didn't say anything. Then Rosie ran over and hugged her.

'Pretty Linda,' she said.

Linda laughed.

'I suppose that settles it,' she said. 'Thanks girls.'

Linda put down the mirror.

'Since you've done such a good job, it seems a pity to be staying in tonight. Why don't we all go out for something to eat? You can come too, Alice, if you like.'

Now what were we supposed to do?

'But ...' I said.

'But ...' said Alice.

'Well?' said Linda.

'But we're cooking dinner here tonight,' I said.

'And we've already bought the food,' added Alice.

Linda sighed.

'That doesn't matter. You can save that food and have a surprise dinner ready tomorrow night when your parents get home.'

I gulped. Mum *would* get a surprise if she came home and saw that there was ready-made lasagne for dinner. And it wouldn't be a pleasant surprise either. She'd go totally crazy, and go on about the dangers of ready-made foods for weeks. It just wouldn't be worth it.

And besides, what about Linda and Peter's romantic date?

I looked at Alice in a panic. She just smiled sweetly.

'Thanks, Linda,' she said. 'But you've been so kind to us, taking us into town, and buying us those lovely t-shirts. We want to repay you by cooking a lovely meal for you.'

Now I started to feel really guilty. Alice was right – Linda *had* been really kind to us, and instead of being grateful we were tricking her into a romatic date. Before I could think of anything to say, Linda shook her head.

'Girls these days,' she said. 'I'd have thought you'd be glad of a night out. But suit yourselves. We'll eat here if that's what you want.'

Alice looked at me.

'That's exactly what we want,' she said. 'Now we'll go away and leave you alone, so you can rest.'

Now Linda looked really puzzled.

'Why on earth would I want to rest?'

Alice laughed a forced kind of laugh.

'What I meant is that you should relax for a while. To let your make-up set.'

Linda looked at Alice like she thought she was crazy, but she only said,

'Come on Rosie. Let's go watch some more TV. We've only watched three hours so far today.'

'Yippee, more telly!' shouted Rosie, and raced into the TV room.

I'm only twelve, but at that moment I felt very old. Life is much simpler when you are only four.

Chapter seventeen

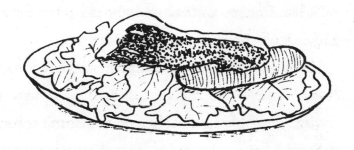

Alice and I spent *ages* getting the dining room ready. We used a lovely white lacy tablecloth and linen serviettes that Alice 'borrowed' from her house. Then we got out all Mum's best dishes and glasses, and the silver cutlery she got for a wedding present, and set the table for two. We picked some flowers from our garden, and put them on the table in a pretty vase. We put the candle we usually only use at Christmas next to the flowers. (And then I had to take it away when I remembered that we'd told Linda that Mum doesn't allow candles in the house.)

We couldn't let Linda see what we were doing because she'd wonder why there were only two place settings, so we had to make her promise to stay out of the room until dinnertime.

Just when we were finished setting the table, Rosie came in to the dining room. At first I thought it would be OK, because she can't count properly yet – (she says one-three-six-nine-a hundred, and thinks she's very clever.) Unfortunately, she noticed immediately that there was something wrong. She walked round and round the table. She patted the first chair and said 'Megan.' Then she patted the second chair and said 'Linda.' She walked around the table one more time with a worried look on her face.

'Where's *my* seat?' she said.

Alice and I had already decided that having Rosie around wouldn't help the 'romantic atmosphere' so we were going to give her her tea early, and put her to bed with Alice's portable

DVD player and a stack of cartoon DVDs. (Which would give Rosie a total of about seven hours of TV that day – a record for any member of our family.)

Alice bent down and spoke kindly to her.

'Megan and I are going to give you yummy cereal for your tea. You can have it in the kitchen. OK?'

Rosie jumped up and down.

'Yummy cereal,' she squealed. 'Lots and lots of yummy cereal.'

I sighed. Mum would think it was child cruelty to send Rosie to bed without a 'proper dinner.' If she ever found out, I'd be in serious trouble.

But what was I supposed to do?

The romantic date wasn't for hours yet, and already things were getting out of hand.

*　　*　　*

When Rosie was full of cereal, and safely in bed with her DVDs, Alice and I started to prepare the salad. Alice was too lazy to wash the lettuce.

'It's from your mum's garden. It doesn't need to be washed,' she said. 'No chemicals, so it's perfectly safe.'

I didn't argue. I was too worried about the whole night to be fussing about a few lettuce leaves.

We put the lettuce on two of Mum's best china plates. It looked a bit bare and lonely – a bit like something you'd feed to a very small and not-very-hungry rabbit. We checked the fridge, but I couldn't see anything else suitable for a salad. Alice spied the rashers and sausages Linda had bought that morning.

'Perfect,' she said. 'I saw a rasher and sausage salad on telly once. It's the latest thing.'

It sounded totally gross to me, but what did I care?

I wasn't going to have to eat it.

I got out the frying pan, and started to fry the rashers and sausages. I decided to cook them all because I was starving, (and besides, we had to get all that evil food out of the house before Mum got back and realised how many of her healthy-eating rules were being broken).

Alice and I ate most of the rashers and sausages, saving one of each for each plate of salad. Then Alice spent ages arranging them on top of the leaves. When she was finished they still looked a bit stupid, but I didn't say anything. Maybe they'd taste better than they looked.

Just as Alice was putting the salads in to the fridge, the doorbell rang.

Suddenly I felt kind of sick. I *so* did not want to be part of what was going to happen next. Maybe I could say I had a tummy-ache and needed to go to bed for the night. I was still wondering if I was brave enough to say this, when Alice grabbed me, and dragged me into the family room where Linda was sitting.

We all looked at each other for a minute. Then Alice poked me, and I said the line I'd been practising in my head.

'Er, Linda,' I said. 'Would you mind getting the door? Alice and I are kind of busy.'

'Sure thing,' Linda said as she jumped up and went out into the hall. Alice and I peeped around the door to see what happened next.

Linda opened the door.

'Oh, hi Peter,' she said. 'Are you looking for Alice? She's just ...'

Peter looked kind of puzzled.

'No, I'm...'

Then he gave a sudden laugh.

'Oh, you're joking. Ha, ha. Funny one.'

Linda didn't laugh with him. She flicked the hall light switch, and the hall suddenly brightened.

'The lights are still working fine,' she said.

'Good,' said Peter. 'I'm glad to hear it.'

Then there was a very long, embarrassing silence. Peter stood on the doorstep, and Linda stood inside the door, looking at him. Alice and I stood behind the family room door, looking at each other.

Finally Linda spoke again.

'Er ... would you like to come in?'

Alice poked me in the ribs and grinned.

'See?' she whispered. 'I told you it would work.'

Peter seemed very relieved.

'Well, why not? Since I'm here.'

Alice and I backed away from the door and tried to look casual. Peter and Linda came into the family room and sat down. Linda made a face at me. I knew she was trying to say *what's going on here?* I put my head down and pretended not to notice.

There was another long silence. This was *sooo* embarrassing.

I tried to catch Alice's eye, but she was busy admiring one of Mum's ornaments on the mantelpiece.

'Maybe Peter would like something to drink,' I suggested, after what seemed like hours of silence. 'There's some orange juice in the fridge.'

'Good idea,' said Linda, sounding relieved. 'Bring a glass for each of us, there's a good girl.'

I spent as long as I could in the kitchen, pouring out the juice *veeeery* slowly and adding ice to it, one small cube at a time. When I got back to the family room, Linda and Peter sipped their orange juice, and looked at Alice and me so often that I began to get really nervous.

Linda and Peter said lots of stupid stuff like – *'That's very nice juice'*, and *'Yes, it is nice, isn't it?'* and *'It's my favourite brand'* and *'I don't much like the juice with the bits in it, do you?'* and *'I don't mind the bits as long as they're not too big.'*

After a long discussion about bits in orange juice, Linda and Peter started to talk about whether it was better to hang rolls of toilet paper with the loose bits hanging on the outside, or on the side close to the wall. I've never been on a romantic date, but if I ever do go on one, I hope it's a bit more interesting than this one was turning out to be. (And I certainly hope I don't end up talking about toilet paper.)

After a while I couldn't take any more. I got up and I went into the kitchen and waited for Alice to follow me.

I didn't have to wait long. Alice was standing beside me in about twenty-five seconds.

'Are they still talking about toilet paper?' I asked.

Alice shook her head.

'No. They've moved on to something much more interesting.'

'What?' I asked.

Alice started to giggle.

'They're talking about the best way to get the gross, black, mouldy stuff off shower curtains.'

I started to laugh too.

'Very romantic. Not,' I said.

'It's early yet,' said Alice. 'Just you wait.'

I folded my arms. Suddenly I didn't feel like laughing any more. This whole thing was totally stupid.

'What exactly are we waiting for?' I asked. 'How are we going to get from mouldy shower curtains to a romantic dinner for two? Linda's sitting there wondering why Peter won't go home and let us get on with our dinner, and Peter's sitting there wondering why she's invited him for dinner when there's no sign of food.'

Alice just smiled.

'Don't panic, Meg.' She said. 'It'll work itself out. One of them will crack sooner or later. I bet it will be Dad. He's always hungry, so he'll mention food before too long, and Linda will be too polite not to invite him to eat, and then they'll be enjoying our delicious food so much, they'll never figure out the truth. It's simple, I promise. Completely simple.'

'Simple'. That awful word again. There should be a law against it, there really should.

Chapter eighteen

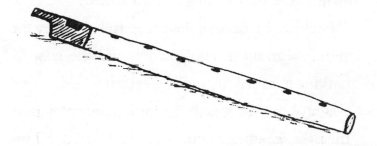

Alice and I went back into the family room and sat together on an armchair. Peter and Linda were talking about the cost of parking in Limerick, compared to Dublin and Cork. If they kept on like this I was sure I'd get so bored I'd fall fast asleep. (And with a bit of luck, I might sleep so long that when I woke up this totally awful night would be over.)

Soon Peter started to seem restless. He was jiggling his feet, and re-arranging himself on the couch. He opened and re-tied his shoelaces three times, and twice he took off his watch and put it back on again.

Linda didn't seem very happy either. She was fiddling with her glass, running her finger around the rim making it hum softly.

Besides the orange juice, the toilet paper, the shower-curtain-mould-cleaner, and the cost of parking in every city in the western world, they'd talked about the weather, tennis, gardening, and then the weather again.

Finally Peter sniffed the air like a puppy-dog trying to find something it had lost. Luckily there was still a strong smell of rashers and sausages.

'Something smells nice,' he said.

'That'll be dinner,' said Linda. 'Alice and Megan are cooking tonight.'

'Yum,' Peter said. 'I can't wait. I'm so hungry you wouldn't believe it.'

Linda gave him a funny look.

He smiled at her.

'I haven't eaten since lunchtime – I've been

saving myself. Don't tell me what we're having – I want it to be a surprise.'

Now Linda looked really puzzled. She gave me another *what's going on?* look. Suddenly Linda reminded me a bit of my mum – a thought so scary that I had to jump up and race back into the kitchen, where she couldn't see me. Alice raced after me, and as we went I could hear Linda's voice behind us.

'Peter … would you … er … I mean maybe … what I'm trying to say is … would you like to stay for something to eat?'

Peter's 'yes' sounded very strange and quiet. The poor man must have been totally confused. As far as he knew, he'd been invited for dinner since earlier in the day, so why on earth would Linda be asking him again? Still, he'd been Alice's dad for over twelve years by now, so if he had any sense he'd have figured out that she must have had something to do with whatever was going on.

Anyway, I didn't have time to worry too much about it, as Alice grabbed me and gave me a high-five that made the palm of my hand sting like crazy.

'Told you,' she hissed. 'Told you they'd crack. Now let's get dinner served before they cop on. You go in and call them.'

I went back into the family room. Linda looked very cross.

'I think I need to have a word with you, Megan,' she said.

'Sure,' I said, trying not to sound scared. 'Maybe later though, I'm kind of busy right now.'

Linda took a long, deep breath. She looked crosser than I had ever seen her before.

'Now is good for me,' she said.

I couldn't think what to say, so I pretended I hadn't heard her.

'May I show you to your table?' I said.

By now both Linda and Peter were looking like there was something very fishy going on, but neither of them said anything – they just got up and followed me into the dining room.

I know we weren't planning to kill anyone or anything, but all of a sudden I felt like what Alice and I were doing was very wrong. I tried to look brave as I waved Linda and Peter to the table, but my hand was shaking so much it spoiled the effect a bit.

Both adults looked at the table, so beautifully set for two, and they spoke at once. 'Why aren't you girls eating?' they said – almost like they'd been practising.

I had actually been rehearsing the answer to this, but my words didn't come out as smoothly and as easily as theirs had.

'Er, I mean... Em... actually... well... you see... Alice and I were really hungry, and with all the food around we couldn't resist... so we ate earlier, and Rosie was tired so we fed her too and put her to bed ... ... so it's just you two now.'

Peter and Linda looked at me like I was totally

crazy, but at least they sat down without asking any more awkward questions.

Just then Alice came in carrying the plates of salad. She put one in front of each adult.

'My speciality,' she said. 'Salad *á la* rashers and sausages. Eat up before it gets cold…er.'

Linda and Peter didn't look very impressed, and I didn't blame them. The lettuce had gone all limp and floppy, and the rashers and sausages were covered in thick, white grease. Still, they obediently picked up their knives and forks.

Alice and I went back into the kitchen, but we lurked near the doorway and listened as our guests ate. For a few minutes all I could hear was the scraping of cutlery, and the squeaky sound of soggy lettuce being chewed – not very pleasant sounds, but at least it meant things were going sort of OK.

Just then there was a sudden, horrible shriek.

'Euuuurgh! What is it? It's *so* disgusting. Get it away from me!'

Alice and I ran back into the room. Linda had jumped up and away from the table, and was cowering in the corner like there was a monster in the room. Peter was poking at the remains of her salad. Finally he found what he was looking for.

'It's just a slug,' he said.

'*Just* a slug,' repeated Linda in a high-pitched voice. 'There's no such thing as "just a slug". It's revolting.'

Peter spoke softly.

'Well, it's not particularly pleasant, I'll admit that. But it won't hurt you. Slugs are perfectly harmless creatures. Anyway, there's only one thing worse than finding a slug in your dinner.'

'What's that?' asked Linda.

Peter laughed.

'Finding half a slug.'

Linda wiped her mouth frantically with the back of her hand, but she did give a small giggle, which vanished quickly as Peter poked a bit more and said,

'Oh dear, speaking of half-slugs....'

Linda looked like she was going to faint.

'I'm joking!' said Peter, but she didn't seem to hear him.

She grabbed a serviette and used it to wipe her tongue, saying stuff like *'grossest thing ever'* and *'I'll have nightmares about this for weeks.'*

Alice raced over and grabbed both salad plates.

'Well, that's starters finished. Please take your places again, and main course will be here before you know it.'

Linda sat back at the table without saying another word. She was a bit pale. I wondered if she was in shock. (If I was really a Guide, I'd probably have known about that kind of stuff, but since I wasn't, I decided to ignore it.)

Back in the kitchen, Alice dumped the salad and slug remains in the bin, then turned to me.

'OK. So you were right again,' she said. 'Maybe we should have washed the lettuce. We'll know better the next time.'

I made a face.

'There won't *be* a next time, Alice. I can promise you that.'

Alice shrugged.

'Whatever. We haven't time to go into that now. Let's forget all about those stupid salads and move on. Now it's time to put the lasagne in the micro—.'

She stopped and slapped the palm of her hand to her head.

'But of course you don't have a microwave, do you?'

I shook my head.

'Not the last time I checked.'

Alice grabbed the lasagne packets and headed for the back door.

'I'll have to run home to heat these up. I'll be as quick as I can. You just go in there and keep them entertained, and whatever happens, don't let them find out that this is a set up.'

Alice was gone for *ages*. I tried every topic of conversation I could think of (including shower-curtain cleaners), but everything seemed to end after one or two sentences. Peter kept looking at his watch and saying how late it was getting, and Linda had a strange look on her face that I couldn't make any sense of.

In the end, out of desperation, I went to my schoolbag, got my tin whistle and my book of songs and started to play. At first Peter and Linda seemed interested. They tapped their feet, and they even clapped at the end of the first two tunes.

By the third tune, their smiles weren't quite as bright and the foot tapping had come to a sudden end.

By the time I heard Alice coming in the back door, I was on the tenth and last tune in my song-book. (That's 'Edelweiss', and it's really hard.) I kept missing notes, and making mistakes. When I got to the end of the song, there were plenty of scuffling noises from the kitchen, but still Alice hadn't appeared. Linda was trying to hide a yawn, and Peter looked as if he had fallen asleep. I decided I'd better play the chorus again.

I was playing the chorus to 'Edelweiss' for the fifth time when Alice finally appeared, holding two plates.

'It's an awful cheat,' she whispered as she went past. 'These lasagnes are a lot smaller than they look on the packet.'

She was right. Each one looked about the right size to fill up a not-very-hungry baby hamster, (who hadn't had a slug and salad starter).

Alice dropped a plate in front of each of our guests. Linda and Peter both brightened up at the sight of the food, so I escaped into the kitchen for a while to catch my breath.

It was turning into a very, very long night.

Chapter nineteen

A lice and I stayed in the kitchen for ages. We could hear Peter and Linda chatting in the living room, so we decided it was best to leave them alone. (Even if they were only talking about mouldy-shower-curtain-cleaners.) Once or twice we could even hear them laughing, and Alice rewarded me with a poke in the ribs that really hurt.

Much later, when my side was black and blue, there was silence in the dining room. Alice put her ear to the door.

'What do you think's going on?' she said.

I really didn't care anymore.

'Dunno. Maybe they're snogging.'

Alice shuddered.

'No need for that. It's their first date, remember? Maybe they've just run out of things to say.'

I giggled.

'Maybe they've decided which is the best shower curtain cleaner in the world.'

Alice giggled too, but only for a second. Then she went all serious again.

'Maybe we should bring in the dessert,' she said.

As she spoke she opened the freezer and rooted around a bit. Then she turned back to me.

'All I can find is packets of spinach. Where did you put the ice-cream?'

I shook my head.

'Nowhere. I thought you put it away.'

'But I thought *you* put it away.'

Five minutes later we found the ice cream in a bag under the kitchen table. I carefully opened the tub, and dipped my finger in. It was like dipping my finger into cream-coloured slime. I sucked my finger.

'Tastes nice,' I said. 'But it isn't exactly ice-cream any more.'

Alice stamped her foot. I decided I really needed to talk to her about that stupid foot-stamping habit. At twelve, she was really a bit old for that kind of thing. (But if she was cross enough to be stamping her foot, that probably meant it wasn't a very good time.)

'Now what?' said Alice. 'I don't suppose your mother has anything else suitable for dessert stashed in her cupboards?'

I laughed.

'Fat chance. Porridge maybe. Or some of that

spinach, but dessert – I don't think so. We've already eaten all the nice stuff that Linda brought.'

'Maybe I could run next door? Or down to the shop?' Alice suggested.

Now it was my turn to stamp my foot. (It felt kind of good, actually.)

'No way,' I said. 'You're not leaving me on my own with those two again. I don't know any more tin whistle tunes.'

'Oh, well,' sighed Alice. 'We'll just have to improvise. Pass me two nice glasses, will you?'

I watched as she slowly and carefully poured the liquid ice cream into the two best glasses I had been able to find.

'What's that meant to be?' I asked.

'Vanilla soup. It's the latest thing in Paris.'

'Really?'

Alice laughed. 'No, but it would be if anyone thought of it.'

I had to laugh too. Messing around in the

kitchen with Alice was fun.

I wished we could forget all about Linda and Peter in the next room.

I wished we could have fun that didn't involve crazy plans.

I wished things could be like they used to be.

Alice stood back and admired her work.

'It needs a finishing touch. Got any coffee to sprinkle on the top?' she asked.

I opened the coffee jar.

'Just coffee beans,' I said, 'and I don't think they're very sprinkly.'

She reached in to the jar and took a few beans.

'They'll do fine.'

Alice dropped the beans on top of the vanilla soup. They stayed there for about a second, and then sank slowly beneath the surface.

Alice made a face.

'I've had a long night. I'm not spending ten minutes fishing for coffee beans,' she said. 'They can still be decorations – invisible decorations.'

I smiled.

'The latest thing in Vienna, I bet.'

Alice smiled back at me. Then she handed me one of the glasses and led the way into the dining room. Luckily, Linda and Peter weren't snogging – that would have been too gross. They were just sitting looking at each other, and saying nothing.

'Dessert is served,' I said.

'Vanilla soup,' said Alice.

'The latest thing in Paris,' I added.

'Indeed?' said Linda, as she pushed the dinner plates to one side.

Peter didn't say anything. He just dived in to his dessert at once, digging into the glass with his spoon. He was probably starving after the half-eaten salad, and the baby-hamster-sized portion of lasagne he'd just had.

He looked really happy for about ten seconds, and then he dropped his spoon, and grabbed his jaw.

'Ooooh! Ouch! What's in this? I nearly broke

my tooth.'

'Secret ingredient,' said Alice. 'If I told you I'd have to kill you.'

Then she grabbed my arm, and dragged me back to the kitchen.

'What if his tooth really is broken?' I asked.

Alice shrugged.

'Don't worry. His tooth isn't broken. He's just being a baby.'

Maybe she was right. All was quiet again in the dining room.

'See?' said Alice. 'He's better already. Now help me with this.'

We put the champagne and two glasses onto Mum's best silver tray. When we went back into the dining room, Linda looked at us in surprise.

'Champagne?' she said. 'What are we celebrating?'

I had to think about that one. I had lots of ideas, but none that seemed suitable to share with Linda.

The fact that you didn't actually eat the slug?

The fact that it looks like Peter didn't break his tooth on that coffee bean after all?

The fact that, despite our best efforts, Alice and I haven't poisoned you?

Alice interrupted my thoughts.

'We're celebrating the fact that it's Saturday night, and we're all here together having a lovely time.'

Ha! – maybe Alice was having a lovely time, but if so she was on her own. I was having a *rotten* time, worrying that everything was going wrong, and it didn't look like Linda and Peter were having much fun either.

Peter reached for the champagne.

'Will I open this?' he said.

Alice grabbed it from his reach.

'No you're the guest. Anyway, it's easy-peasy – I've seen this done on TV hundreds of times.'

She carefully peeled back the foil, and then she took off the cute little wire cage that surrounded the cork. Then she used her thumbs to ease the cork from the bottle. It came out slowly, like toothpaste from a nearly empty tube. When the cork was almost out, Alice suddenly shoved the bottle into my hands.

'Here. You do it,' she said. 'I'm too afraid. And I hate loud noises.'

I was afraid too, but it was too late to do anything about it. I felt like I was holding a hand-grenade, or a bomb that was just about to go off. I held the bottle as far away from my body as I could, wishing that my arms were a bit longer.

Alice ducked behind a chair, Linda covered her eyes, and Peter called,

'Careful with that.'

Too late – there was a huge loud pop, and the cork shot from the bottle like a bullet. It whizzed across the room, and managed to find Mum's favourite crystal vase, which was supposedly safe on the top shelf of the cabinet. The vase toppled for a second, then rocked, and then danced into the air. I didn't know whether to cover my eyes or my ears. There was a huge crash, and then a chorus of *oh no's* from Linda, Peter and Alice. I raced over. The vase was broken into about a hundred pieces – about ninety-eight too many for superglue to be of any use.

I put my head down. I felt like crying.

Why had I let Alice bully me into this?

Now I was going to be in huge trouble, and all for nothing. Linda was glaring at Alice, and Peter was looking more embarrassed than ever.

Just then Rosie appeared in the doorway.

'Big bang?' she said.

She went and stood next to Linda.

'Oh, you poor little poppet,' Linda said. 'Did the loud noise wake you up? And look at you, you're all wet. Is it too warm in your bedroom? Are you sweating from the heat?'

Even Rosie was embarrassed now.

Why couldn't Linda get the smell?

Had the vanilla soup gone to her head?

Was she wearing too much perfume?

The damp patch on Rosie's nightie wasn't because her room was too hot. I should have warned Linda that one of Mum's ten thousand rules actually made sense. It really wasn't clever to give Rosie anything to drink after seven o'clock.

Still, I had enough problems without worrying about that.

I winced as Linda pulled Rosie onto her knee and cuddled her. That, I supposed, was definitely that. If there was any hope of a romance between Linda and Peter, surely a wee-wee soaked child would put an end to it for good?

I looked wearily at Alice.

'Come on,' I said. 'I'll take Rosie upstairs and get her changed into something dry. I suppose you might as well get started on the washing up.'

Chapter twenty

When Rosie was clean and dry again, she didn't want to go back to bed.

'No,' she said, stamping her little bare foot and sounding a lot like Alice. 'I'm going back downstairs to sit on Linda's knee!'

I sighed. It probably didn't matter. The night was ruined anyway. So I let Rosie run down to Linda, and I went to help Alice with the washing-up.

Much later, when the kitchen was finally clean,

Alice stood back and looked at me.

'What do you think?' she said.

'About what?' I asked. (Like I didn't know what she was talking about.)

'About the night? Do you think it was a success?'

I shrugged.

'Well, we didn't burn the house down, which is always a good thing.'

Alice stamped her foot.

'Be serious, Megan. What do you think about the romantic date? Do you think it worked? Do you think Dad will tell Mum that he's met someone else? Do you think Mum will get jealous?'

I sighed. As far as I could tell, the whole thing had been a complete disaster, almost as bad as the trip to Fota Island with Miss O'Herlihy had been. I didn't want to disappoint Alice though.

'It's hard to tell with adults,' I said. 'Linda and your dad seemed to get on OK … sort of … I suppose.'

Alice put down the tea towel she had been fiddling with.

'Oh, forget it, Meg,' she said. 'Thanks for trying to protect me, but I know it was a total mess. Dad and Linda are probably in there wondering how on earth they can escape without hurting the other person's feelings. I think I'll just go in there and put them out of their misery. I'll tell Dad I want him to bring me home.'

She opened the door into the dining room, half-stepped in, and then stepped back out again.

'Look,' she whispered.

I leaned around her and looked into the room. Linda and Peter had moved to the sofa, and were sitting with their backs to us. From the way they were sitting, it looked like they were already best buddies.

Linda said something I couldn't quite catch, and Peter laughed like it was the funniest thing he'd ever heard in his whole life. After a minute he wiped his eyes and said,

'You know, Linda, this has been such a great evening. Since Veronica and I … I mean since … well … since my marriage broke up, I haven't gone out very much. I suppose I've just been sitting at home feeling sorry for myself. I should make more of an effort.'

'Well,' replied Linda. 'I'm glad you made the effort tonight. I'm so glad you just took the notion to drop over this evening.'

I gulped. So this was it. This was the moment when Linda and Peter finally understood what had happened. There was a long silence during which I could hear my heart beating really fast. Then Peter spoke. His voice was puzzled.

'But …' he began.

Linda interrupted him. 'And it's so lucky you hadn't eaten before you got here.'

Alice and I made faces at each other as we backed in further behind the kitchen door. This was the moment I had been dreading ever since

Alice told me about her stupid plan.

Now Peter sounded really puzzled.

'But why would I have eaten, when you …'

He stopped speaking and scratched his head.

'When I what?' asked Linda.

'Forget it,' said Peter. 'It's nothing. We had a very nice evening, so why don't we leave it at that?'

I was just breathing a lovely, long, happy sigh of relief when Linda spoke again.

'No really, Peter. I'd like to know. What were you going to say?'

I held my breath again, and then Peter answered.

'What I'm trying to say is, why would I have eaten before coming over here, since you already had invited me for dinner?'

There was a long, long silence. My heart was beating harder and faster than ever. I wondered if it had ever happened that someone's heart beat so hard that it jumped right out of their chest and rolled around on the floor in front of them.

Then Peter spoke again.

'I'm sorry, Linda,' he said. 'But you *did* plan this evening? You *did* send the girls over to invite me for dinner this morning, didn't you?'

Now Linda sat up straight.

'Er, well, not exactly. You see Megan and Alice said…'

Now Peter jumped up from his seat.

'Megan. And Alice. Those two girls. I should have known there was something fishy going on. What on earth are they up to this time?'

By now Alice and I were out of sight, squashed right in behind the door. Peter sounded really cross, and there was no way I was going out there to face him.

Now Peter really raised his voice.

'I am going to sort Alice out for once and for all. This time she's gone too far. She really has. Alice, come out here right now.'

I looked at Alice. She shook her head. 'I'm not going out there,' she whispered. 'He'll kill me.'

So what exactly was she planning to do? Stay hidden behind my kitchen door for the rest of her life?

Suddenly Linda started to laugh.

Peter sounded kind of irritated.

'What's so funny?'

Linda was really laughing now. 'You've got to hand it to those girls. They really are very inventive. They rightly set us up. Inviting you over for dinner, without telling me, and cooking all that er, *interesting* food.'

Peter gave a small laugh.

'But what were they thinking of? Why on earth did they go to all this trouble?'

'I haven't the faintest idea,' said Linda. 'And I don't really care either. It's exactly like the kind of thing I would have loved to do when I was a little girl. Except I was always too scared.'

Peter sighed.

'I was a timid little boy myself,' he said.

Linda laughed again.

'Anyway, don't you agree that the whole thing was a bit of fun? And we had a good time – much better than sitting watching TV for the evening.'

Peter still wasn't happy.

'But why?' he asked again. 'What was this whole thing supposed to be about?'

'Oh, you know girls,' replied Linda.

Peter sounded sad.

'That's the problem, I suppose. I don't really know much about girls at all.'

Linda laughed again.

'Well, pour us another glass of champagne, and I'll let you into a few secrets.'

There was the clink of glasses, and then Peter and Linda's voices got so low we couldn't make out anything more.

A few minutes later, Al and I peeped around the door again. Peter and Linda were still sitting side by side on the sofa. As we watched, Peter leaned over, until his face was right next to Linda's.

Alice covered her eyes.

'He's going to kiss her,' she gasped.

'But that's what you wanted, isn't it?' I said.

Alice shook her head.

'Yes. I mean no. I mean I don't know.'

Just then Rosie popped her head over the couch.

'Hi Meg. Hi Alice,' she said. 'Guess what? I need to do another wee.'

If there ever was going to be a kiss, that put a quick end to it. Peter leaped away from the couch like it was on fire, and Linda grabbed Rosie and took her upstairs.

When Linda got back, with Rosie in her arms, Peter stood up.

'I think it's about time I went home,' he said. 'Thank you so much for a wonderful evening. Come on, Alice. Let's go home, and you and I can discuss the lovely *invitation* to dinner that you gave me this morning.'

Alice made a face at me, and followed him out the door.

I went to the front door and watched as Alice and her dad made their way home.

Poor Alice – she was so mixed up lately.

And poor me – I had to go back inside to face Linda.

Chapter twenty-one

When I got back inside Linda had put Rosie on the couch, and was tucking a cosy blanket around her. When Rosie was nicely settled, and almost asleep, Linda turned to me with her arms folded. She didn't look very cross, but she didn't look very happy either. I was starting to feel very uncomfortable.

'Let's clear up a bit,' I said, and I picked up the two empty champagne glasses and headed for the kitchen.

I guessed that Linda would follow me – and I was right. We both sat at the kitchen counter and looked at each other. Linda's make-up had worn off, and she was back to her old self – the self I was used to.

I just wished she wouldn't keep looking at me like that.

In the end the silence got to me.

'I suppose I'm in the biggest trouble ever,' I said.

Linda thought for a minute.

'Nobody died I suppose.'

I couldn't help giggling.

'Someone could have. Alice and I are really bad cooks.'

I was very relieved when Linda laughed too.

'Vanilla soup – that was a first for me. And a last too I hope.'

Then she got serious again.

'OK, Megan,' she said. 'Here's the deal. You tell me exactly what this was all about, and then you don't get into big trouble. How about that?'

I *so* did not want to tell Linda about the plan, but it didn't sound like I had much choice. Maybe if I told her the truth, she'd be able to understand why I had to help Alice.

'Well,' I began. 'You see, it's like this – you know Alice's mum and dad don't live together any more?'

Linda nodded and I continued.

'Well, we thought that if you and Peter, sort of…….'

I stopped talking. Now that I was trying to explain it to someone else, it sounded really, *really* stupid. How had Alice ever persuaded me to join in this crazy plan?

Linda urged me on.

'If Peter and I what?'

I spoke in a big rush.

'Alice thought that if you and Peter kind of fell in love, Veronica, that's Alice's mum, would get jealous, and then she'd try to get back with Peter, and they could all live happily ever after.'

Linda spoke very quietly – so quietly that I had to lean forward to try to catch what she was saying.

'And what about Peter? Did you think about his feelings at all?'

I shook my head. I'd been so busy worrying about not getting into trouble, I hadn't really thought about Peter at all.

Linda continued.

'Your mum told me all about Peter before. Things were difficult between him and Veronica for ages. He's had a very hard time since she left. What if he fell madly in love with me, and then I turned around and went back to Dublin? Did you think about that at all?'

I shook my head again. This was awful. Linda wasn't being cross – she was even being quite nice – but she was making me feel like I'd been a total idiot.

Linda wasn't finished yet.

'And what about me? You and Alice were just using me, weren't you?'

I nodded slowly. I hadn't really thought of it like that, but now that she mentioned it, I knew she was right.

Linda went on.

'What if I fell madly in love with Peter? What then?'

I covered my face. I'd never even thought of that happening.

'Would you…… I mean did you… I mean…?'

Linda sighed.

'Peter's a very nice man,' she said. 'And we had a lovely evening together, but…'

Linda stopped talking, and then started again.

'Let's forget about Peter for one minute,' she said. 'I've just remembered the makeover you and Alice gave me this afternoon.'

I put my head down. I could feel my face going red. Linda gently put her finger under my chin, and lifted it so I was looking right into her eyes.

'That makeover wasn't a Guide project was it?' she asked.

I shook my head slowly.

'You're not even in the Guides, are you?'

I shook my head again – even slower this time.

'And that thing with the lights not working last night – did you and Alice have something to do with that?' she asked.

I nodded.

There was a very long silence. This was so, so awful. Linda is always so nice to me, and now she knew that I'd told her loads of lies.

Suddenly Linda started to laugh.

'You girls,' she said. 'What are you like?'

I couldn't laugh with her. I still felt too bad. Linda was my aunt, and what if she really had fallen in love with Peter? It would have been all my fault. I should never have let Alice talk me into this stupid plan. I could feel tears coming to my eyes.

'I'm sorry,' I said. 'I'm really, really sorry. For everything. And Linda, do you... I mean... Peter... do you ... do you like him?'

To my great relief, Linda shook her head.

'As I said before, Peter's a very nice man, but he's not my type. Not my type at all. And...'

Linda stopped speaking and gave a funny little smile that made me crazy to know what she'd been planning to say.

'Go on,' I urged her. 'And what?'

Now Linda was beaming. She lowered her voice again, even though, besides the two of us, there was only Rosie in the house, and she was surely asleep by now.

'And ... can you keep a secret?'

I nodded. I *love* secrets. (Except for the ones that Alice tells me, which always get me into trouble.)

'I met this man in Dublin a few months ago,'

said Linda. 'He's nice. Well actually, he's more than that – he's *very* nice. And maybe, some day … well, let's just say I have a good feeling about this.'

This was fantastic news.

'Does Mum know about this?' I asked.

Linda shook her head.

'No, and you're not to tell her either. You know what she's like. If she hears a word about it, she'll get all excited, and she'll probably start knitting me a wedding dress or crocheting a bouquet of flowers or something. I'll tell her soon, I promise. But don't say a word just yet.'

I laughed.

'OK. It can be our little secret.'

We didn't say anything for a while. It was so cool, Linda having a boyfriend at last. She must have been lonely in Dublin on her own for all those years.

I wondered if she was going to get married. Maybe she'd ask me to be her bridesmaid. Being a bridesmaid would be so totally cool. And Rosie would make a really cute flower girl. And Mum would never buy a new outfit, I knew that for sure, but at least she still had the nice pale green dress from my Confirmation, and she could wear that to the wedding. We could all go to a fancy hotel and…

Linda interrupted my happy thoughts, and dragged me back to the present.

'I suppose the whole dinner date thing was Alice's idea,' she said.

I nodded.

'Since her parents split up, Alice and I never do normal stuff any more. All she does is come up with crazy plans to try to get them back together.'

'The poor little thing,' said Linda. 'She must be really unhappy.'

'She doesn't always say it, but I know she is,' I said. 'And sometimes I feel like telling her just to stop making a fuss, and get on with it. And sometimes that makes me feel really mean. After all – what do I know about what it's like to be Alice? Mum and Dad drive me crazy most of the time, but at least they're happy together.'

Linda nodded. Suddenly I had to have her opinion.

'What do you think about this plan?' I asked. 'This "romantic date" between you and Peter? Do you think it might work? Do you think Alice's mum might get jealous, and get back together with her dad?'

Linda smiled.

'Well, Alice is a plucky kid, and I can't blame her for trying. But even if Alice's mum does feel slightly jealous, that might not make her want to get back together with Peter.'

'What do you mean?' I asked.

This time Linda thought for ages before she answered.

'Well, sometimes things are a lot more compli-cated than kids understand. Sometimes, if something is broken badly enough, it can never be fixed, no matter how hard you try. It's very sad for Alice and her little brother. And it's sad for Peter and Veronica too. But—'

I interrupted her.

'But what about Alice? She still thinks her plan is going to work. She hasn't given up. She *never* gives up.'

Linda gave a long sigh.

'Well, I suppose miracles sometimes do happen.'

I put my head in my hands for a second, and then I looked at Linda again.

'And if there's no miracle?' I asked.

Linda put her arm around me.

'Then you'll just have to continue being a good friend, and be there to help Alice pick up the pieces.'

Chapter twenty-two

When I got up the next morning, the last thing I felt like doing was going over to Alice's. I was kind of afraid, and I didn't know what to say to her.

So instead, I hung around the kitchen for ages, trying to avoid the issue.

'I can't make you go over there,' said Linda. 'But if you don't go, I might ask you to help me clean the house.'

I sighed. Linda had been in Limerick for too long. She was getting more like my mother every day. Still, I thought, maybe vacuuming the house would be more fun than spending time with

Alice after the disaster of the night before. While I was still making up my mind what to do, Linda pushed me out the front door.

'Alice needs you,' she said. 'Continue to be a good friend to her.'

Alice was already up and dressed when I got to her house. She greeted me with a huge, happy smile. What on earth could she be smiling about?

— 'Aren't you in the biggest trouble ever?' I asked.

Alice shrugged.

'No. Why?'

'Because you got your dad to come for dinner in our house, even though he hadn't been invited? Because you set him up? Because ...' I didn't know how to go on.

Alice shrugged again.

'I know. I should be in the biggest trouble ever, but I'm not. Dad should have given me a hard time, but he didn't. He didn't even ask me any questions about last night - about why we did it, or anything. He's just been kind of quiet.'

'That's very strange,' I said.

'I know,' agreed Alice. 'But if I'm not in trouble, I certainly don't plan to ask Dad why.'

'Good idea,' I said, relieved that she was being so calm, and hoping that maybe this was an end to the whole 'romantic date' thing.

Suddenly Alice spoke again.

'Anyway, Meg,' she said. 'I want to thank you.'

I was suspicious.

'For what?' I asked.

Alice smiled again.

'For helping me. I think last night's romantic dinner date was a really big success.'

Hello?

What on earth was she on about?

Had she been in the same house as me last night?

What about the slug, who nearly became a half slug?

The miniature lasagne?

The melted ice cream?

Peter's almost-broken tooth?

The really broken vase that Mum would never, ever forgive me for?

The….

Alice interrupted my thoughts.

'Don't you think it went really well, Meg?'

'Er, how exactly was that?' I asked.

'OK, so the food wasn't all that great, but…….'

I interrupted her.

'The food was worse than "not all that great". It was totally disastrous.'

Alice laughed.

'OK, so the food was practically poisonous, but that doesn't matter now. I've been thinking about this all night – I hardly slept at all. I've decided that what matters is that Dad and Linda really did have a proper date. It was a real dinner, with three courses, and champagne. And later on, when Mum comes over with Jamie, I can tell her all about it.'

'But there's not really anything to tell, is there?' I protested.

'But there *is*. OK, so they didn't end up all lovey-dovey, but you could tell that Dad really had a good time with Linda. They nearly kissed, remember? Once Mum hears about that, she'll start to get worried. I know it.'

I felt I had to stop her. After talking to Linda, I knew that there had never been any question of a kiss.

'Now that I think about it,' I said. 'Maybe your dad and Linda weren't going to kiss last night.'

'So why was he leaning over her like that?'

I thought quickly.

'Maybe he was just trying to get away from Rosie – you know how she wriggles!'

'Yeah, right,' said Alice. 'I'm telling you, Megan. I have a good feeling about this. My plan is going to work. I just know it.'

I was wondering whether I should tell her what Linda had said that morning, when the doorbell rang.

'That'll be Mum,' said Alice as she dragged me into the hall to open the door.

Jamie said 'hi' and ran upstairs. Veronica stepped into the hall.

'Hi, Mum,' said Alice. 'Come on in. How are you? Did you have a nice night?'

Veronica kissed Alice as she passed her, and went to sit in the living room.

'It was very nice thank you,' she said. 'Jamie and I had pizza and then we watched a DVD and had an early night.'

Alice made a face.

'Sounds totally booooring to me,' she said.

'Well then, what did you do that was so exciting?' asked Veronica.

Alice grinned at her.

'It wasn't me who did something exciting. It was Dad. He had a very, very exciting night.'

Veronica sighed.

'Don't tell me – he watched a new TV channel? He bought himself a new pair of socks? He decided to support a new soccer team?'

Now Alice sounded cross.

'Very funny, Mum. Not. He had his big date. Remember? With Linda, Megan's aunt.'

'Oh, that. I'd forgotten all about that,' said Veronica. 'How did he get on?'

It sounded to me like Veronica was interested, but not in a jealous kind of way. Alice didn't seem to notice this. She began to gush.

'Oh, he had the most fantastic time. The date was in Megan's house – but only because Linda had to mind Megan and Rosie. Otherwise they'd have gone to a really posh restaurant. Megan and I cooked dinner – three courses – very fancy. It was *soooo* delicious. Dad loved it. Then they had champagne, and it was *veeeeery* romantic. Wasn't it Megan?'

I jumped.

'Er… yes. I suppose it was,' I said.

'And then Linda and Dad—'

Just then Peter came in to the room.

'Linda and Dad what?'

Alice didn't even blink, but I wondered what she had planned to say next – something totally gross like that Linda and Peter kissed for ages – or something exaggerated like that they were going to get engaged any day now.

'Oh,' Alice said now. 'I was just telling Mum about your date last night.'

Peter grinned and looked at Alice.

'Well, I suppose you could say we had an interesting evening.'

Suddenly I knew I had to get out of there. Since I'd been Alice's friend for so long, I was used to weird stuff, but this was even weirder than usual. I was in her house listening to her mum and dad discussing her dad's hot date with my aunt. I mean really, how weird is that?

I grabbed Alice's arm, and pulled her out of the room.

'Come *on*, Al,' I said. 'I need to talk to you outside. Urgently.'

I had taken Alice by surprise, so I got her as far as the hall before she realised what was happening. There, she dug in her heels and folded her arms and refused to go any further. Since she's bigger and stronger than me, I couldn't force her.

'What do you urgently want to talk to me about?' she asked.

I sighed.

'Anything. I don't care. Let's just get out of here. Let's go to my place and see if Linda has any more secret supplies of chocolate.'

Alice shook her head.

'Sorry, Meg. I'm not going anywhere. I need to listen to Mum and Dad. I need to know what's happening.'

As she spoke, she edged closer to the living room door, pulling me along next to her.

I don't even like eavesdropping. Mum has told

me about a million times how mean and dishonest it is to listen in on other peoples' conversations, and I kind of agree with her. Since Alice's parents broke up, though, I never seemed to do anything else. And what was really scary, I was starting to get good at it.

I held my breath, leaned in closer and listened.

'......and then I went home,' said Peter.

Veronica spoke softly.

'It sounds like you had a lovely evening,' she said. 'I'm happy for you. I really am.'

I looked at Alice. Obviously Veronica wasn't one bit jealous. Now would Alice admit that her plan had failed?

Fat chance.

'Don't worry,' she hissed. 'Mum doesn't mean it. I bet she's really jealous. She just doesn't want Dad to know it.'

Then Peter spoke again.

'You know, Veronica, last night has made me understand something.'

'What's that?' she said.

'Well, it's made me see that I've been afraid to let go of our marriage. I've been hanging on, hoping you're going to change your mind.'

Now Veronica's voice was so soft I could just barely hear it.

'I'm not going to change my mind you know, Peter. It's over for us forever. I'm sorry.'

Peter sighed.

'I know that now. And after spending the evening with Linda, I know I can move on.'

Veronica sounded interested.

'So there's really something between you two?'

Peter shook his head.

'No. Definitely not. Linda's nice, but she really isn't my type. It's just that I enjoyed her company. We had a nice evening, and I realised that it's stupid to sit at home clinging to the past. I think I've finally accepted that our marriage is over.'

I gulped. That was probably the saddest speech I'd ever heard. I looked at Alice. She wasn't making any sound, but streams of tears were pouring down her face and dripping on to her sweatshirt. This was too much for me. I wanted to help her, but I didn't know what to do. This wasn't a problem that could be sorted out with a cup of hot chocolate and a few nice biscuits. This time there was only one place Alice could go to for help.

I gave her a small push towards the living room.

'Go,' I whispered. 'Go in, and talk to them.'

For once in her life, Alice didn't argue with me. She ran in to the living room and threw herself on to the couch between her parents. I watched as they both hugged her and tried to wipe away her tears.

Then I let myself out the back door, and went to sit on one of her swings.

Alice didn't need me right now, but later on, I knew she would.

And when she did, I was going to be right

there, waiting for her.

That's what best friends do – right?

Chapter twenty-three

Much, much later, Alice came out to the garden. Her face was pale, and her eyes were all red and puffy. She sat on the swing beside me and gave me a weak smile.

'Thanks for staying,' she said.

I smiled at her.

'That's OK.'

For a few minutes we were quiet. Without saying anything, we got involved in one of our swinging competitions, trying to see who would be first to hit the branches of the old apple tree with our feet. All I could hear was the creaking of the swing-chains, and the rustling of the leaves in the apple-tree. This swinging competition is one of the few things I'm better than Alice, but this time I let her win. I thought it might make her feel a bit better.

After we'd both kicked the branches a few times, we let our swings slow down, until they were barely moving.

'Well,' Alice said. 'As clever plans go, I suppose that one counts as a bit of a failure.'

'What do you mean?' I asked, as if I didn't know.

'The plan was, we'd get Dad to go out with Linda, Mum would get jealous, she'd fall in love with Dad again, she'd move back in here, and the O'Rourke family would all live happily ever after.

What really happened was, we got Dad to go out with Linda, and as a result he's decided that he and Mum are never getting back together. Ever. It's over, and all the secret plans in the world won't be able to change it.'

I leaned over and stroked her shoulder, not an easy thing to do when you're on a swing.

'I'm sorry, Al,' I said. 'I really am. I should have stopped you. I shouldn't have let you go on with your plan.'

Alice gave a small laugh.

'Yeah, right. Like you should have stopped me when I hid under your bed at Halloween? Like you should have stopped me at spring mid-term, when I tried to get rid of Norman? I know it's not easy to stop me when I have a plan. It's like I get so carried away, I can't see straight any more.'

I had to smile. I'd never have guessed that Alice knew herself so well.

'But this time I should have tried harder,' I said. 'This time I think we made things worse.'

Alice shook her head.

'I don't think so. Mum and Dad were never going to get back together. Even Dad knows that now. And there's no point hoping for something that's never going to happen. It's just stupid. It's like a little kid waking up on St Stephen's Day, sad that he has no more presents to open, and wishing that every day could be Christmas Day.'

'I used to wish that,' I said.

'Me too,' said Alice. 'And every year, I used to wish for a pony for my birthday, but Dad hates animals, and wouldn't even let me get a goldfish, so that was kind of a waste of time.'

Now I laughed.

'That's a bit like wishing that my mum's going to come home one day and say, "Megan, dear, I've decided I've been too strict about food. There's going to be no more vegetables or porridge in this house. It's going to be a diet of sweets and biscuits around here from now on."'

Alice laughed too.

'I think you've got the idea. Sometimes the time comes when it's better to face up to the truth. It's easier in the end.'

I smiled back at her, and started to swing again. It made me a bit sad to see my crazy friend being so calm, so sensible.

After a minute, Alice started to swing too. She gave a sudden giggle.

'Let's think of a really great trick to play on Melissa. We've only got a few weeks left at school, so it's got to be a biggie.'

I gave a sigh of happiness. Alice O'Rourke was never going to be sensible. That was always going to be my job.

Chapter twenty-four

Linda, Rosie and I had yummy pizza for lunch. I ate four *huge* slices, and then stopped, as I felt like my belly was going to burst open, spraying the whole room with pineapple and pepperoni and cheese and tomato sauce.

'Mum never lets us have pizza,' I said, now that it was too late for Linda to do anything about it.

'I know,' said Linda, wiping tomato sauce from her mouth. 'That's why I decided to have it today.'

I sighed.

'Mum is so obsessed with healthy food. It's totally pathetic. I wish she could be a bit more like you.'

Linda smiled across the table at me.

'She only does what she thinks is best for you. It's easy for me. I hardly ever see you, so I can relax and spoil you a bit. Your mum can't do that.'

'Yeah, but if you were my mum, what would you do?'

Linda smiled again.

'Sorry, Megan. I'd probably be just like your mum. I'd fill you up with healthy food, until you were begging for mercy.'

That made me feel a bit better, but I'm not really sure why. Maybe it was the thought that Mum isn't such a freak after all.

Just then the doorbell rang.

'I'll get it,' I said, as I ran into the hall. 'It's probably Alice.'

I opened the door and was very surprised to

see Alice's dad there, holding a large cardboard box with a ribbon on it. I felt like closing the door in his face.

What was he doing here?

I thought Linda 'wasn't his type'.

Did he really think she would be interested in him just because he brought her a big present?

I felt sorry for him, but that didn't mean I wanted him hanging around my house, making my life even more complicated.

'I'll get Linda,' I said.

Peter put his hand up.

'No. Don't, Megan. It's you I want to see.'

I backed away a bit.

Why did Peter want to see me?

Did he think the whole romantic date thing was my idea?

Was he going to tell me to stay away from Alice for the rest of my life?

How unfair would that be?

Peter held the box towards me.

'This is for you,' he said.

I took the box, and stood there holding it, not knowing what to do next.

Peter smiled.

'You can open it, if you like,' he said.

So I carefully balanced the box in one hand and used the other to pull off the ribbon. I opened the lid and looked inside the box. Inside was a crystal vase.

'I think it's the same as the one that got broken last night,' said Peter proudly. 'I spent ages trying to find the exact one. You see, Alice—'

I interrupted him.

'But I'm the one who broke the vase,' I said. 'Not Alice.'

Peter raised his eyebrows.

'OK, so you were the one holding the champagne bottle at the time, but it doesn't take a genius to figure out that the whole sorry mess was Alice's idea.'

He was right, of course, but I felt I ought to try

to defend my friend.

'It wasn't just Alice,' I said. 'I helped too. I—'

Peter put up his hand to interrupt me.

'It's OK, Megan,' he said. 'Whatever you did, I'm sure Alice did ten times more. And she's not in trouble, so you don't have to protect her.'

I gave a small sigh. Since no one was in trouble, it was probably better not to say any more. And besides, having the vase would save me an awful lot of explaining when Mum and Dad got home.

Peter took the box from me again.

'I'll take away the packaging, and you just take the vase, and put it back where the old one used to be, and no-one will ever know the difference.'

I carefully lifted the vase from the box. Inside it was a brown note – fifty euro.

'Look,' I said. 'You left this inside by mistake.'

Peter shook his head.

'That's not a mistake. That's just a little something for you. Buy yourself something nice with it.'

Fifty euro. I closed my eyes and thought of all the cool things I could buy. Maybe Mum would let me go to town with Alice after school one day. We could go for hot chocolate. I could buy new clothes, and Alice could help me pick them out. I'd even have enough to buy something for Alice too. We could have such fun. I opened my eyes and looked at Peter again.

'But why.......?' I began.

Peter smiled at me.

'Alice has had a very hard time of it these past few months, but you've stood by her all the way. I know she can be difficult, but you've stayed with her no matter what. She's a lucky girl to have a friend like you.'

I didn't know what to say to this, so I said nothing. I folded up the money and put it into my pocket. I was embarrassed, and Peter looked like he was going to cry.

He turned away.

'I'll be off so,' he said.

'Good-bye, and thanks,' I said, but I don't think he heard me.

Chapter twenty-five

Linda and I spent ages hiding the evidence of all the rules we had broken over the weekend.

We went to the recycling centre and got rid of all the pizza packages and the Coke bottles and the packets from the brightly-coloured cereals. When we got back we tidied every inch of the house. I put the new vase up on the cabinet, where the old one used to be. When everything was done, Linda took Mum's list of rules and put it back on the kitchen table. She smiled at me.

'Remember, Megan,' she said. 'Your Mum makes these rules for your benefit.'

'So why did you let me disobey them all?' I asked.

She shrugged.

'Oh well, we all need a break now and then. Sometimes it's good to live a little.'

'Linda,' I said suddenly. 'Are you going to tell Mum about last night – about the dinner, and Peter coming over for a date and all that stuff?'

Linda didn't answer for a minute, and I started to feel a bit scared. I should have known adults always back each other up in the end. It's like they have some secret pact they won't let us kids in on.

'Well,' said Linda eventually. 'Are you going to tell your mum about my new friend in Dublin?'

I shook my head, and Linda came over and hugged me.

'That's my girl,' she said. 'You won't tell and I won't tell. Let's call it quits.'

*　　*　　*

Half an hour later, I heard a car outside in the driveway.

Seconds later Mum raced into the house like she was being chased by a pack of mad dogs. She grabbed Rosie and hugged her so tightly I was sure Rosie wouldn't be able to breathe. Then she showered her with huge sloppy kisses.

'My little baby,' she said. 'My poor, sweet, little baby. Did you miss Mummy and Daddy?'

Rosie didn't answer – she was too busy struggling to breathe. I smiled to myself. I was sure Rosie hadn't missed Mum and Dad one tiny bit – she'd been having too much fun, watching TV and eating foods she wasn't usually allowed.

Finally Mum released Rosie, and came rushing over to me. Luckily I was ready for her, so I managed to escape after only one hug and five or six noisy kisses.

'Well, Megan,' she said as I wriggled away. 'How was your weekend? Did you behave yourself for Linda?'

I could feel my face going red, and I looked at Linda.

Linda smiled at me.

'Don't worry,' she told Mum. 'Megan is a great girl, and she was as good as gold all the time you were gone.'

Mum smiled too.

'I'm glad to hear it,' she said.

Just then Dad came in carrying what looked like enough camping stuff to keep a very large army going for about six months. His face was pale, his hair was greasy and he looked like he hadn't slept for the whole weekend.

'Hi girls,' he said. 'Where's my bed? Show me my bed, and I'll lie in it for the rest of the day.'

Linda laughed.

'Didn't you sleep well in Galway?'

Dad shook his head.

'Fat chance,' he said. 'Have you ever tried sleeping on a bed of rocks? Trust me, it's not comfortable. And I haven't had a shower since I left here. I—'

Mum interrupted him.

'That's your own fault,' she said. 'There was a shower there.'

Dad gave a scary kind of laugh.

'Yeah,' he said. 'One shower, between hundreds of people. And it was cold. In my opinion, that's taking concern for the environment one step too far. Anyway, I've made up my mind – I'm never, ever, ever going camping again. I'm too old for that kind of stuff.'

Mum gave him a playful push.

'You're nothing but a big softy,' she said. 'And I've got some bad news for you. We're going to the Foggy Mountain festival every year from now on. It's going to be my annual treat.'

Dad went even paler. 'But the children... .'

Linda interrupted.

'Don't worry. I'll mind Rosie and Megan. Same time next year. We're looking forward to it already, aren't we girls?'

I grabbed Rosie and we danced around the kitchen. Luckily Mum didn't stop to wonder why we were so happy – she was too busy rummaging in her handbag.

'Look girls,' she said. 'I brought you back some treats. Who'd like some organic breadsticks?'

I sighed. It looked like the party was over.

Mum asked Linda to stay for tea, but for some reason Linda didn't seem tempted by the lentil stew and spinach that Mum was offering.

'Thanks, Sheila,' she said. 'But no thanks. I need to get back. I'm meeting ... well, I'm busy.'

As she spoke, she gave me a big wink. I winked back, grinning to myself.

In spite of Alice's crazy plan, it had been a great weekend.

Chapter twenty-six

A few weeks later, Alice came up with a very elaborate plan for a trick we could play on Melissa. It involved lots of phone calls, secret meetings, bags of flour, and water balloons. It was quite a good plan actually (considering Alice had come up with it), but we never got around to carrying it out. We never seemed to find the time.

You see, by this time, we were all getting very excited about going to secondary school. Most of the class were going to move on to the school that was just up the road from our primary school. The twins, Ellen and Emma, were repeating sixth class, and Melissa was going to go to a posh boarding school in Dublin.

At the beginning of the year, Melissa used to bore us all to death bragging about how fancy her new school was going to be.

'All the famous people send their kids there,' she used to say. 'Pop-stars, actors – everyone who matters really. It's *so* expensive, ordinary people just can't afford it. And it's got this totally fantastic swimming pool. We get to use it every day after school, so I'm glad I've been going to swimming lessons since I was three. At Easter we all get to go to France on an exchange trip, and we …'

On and on and on she went every day until we all felt like we'd throw up if we heard one more word about it.

Now, as the summer holidays approached, Melissa began to talk less and less about her fancy boarding school.

Alice was the first to notice. She mentioned it one day at break-time.

'Anyone hear anything lately about the best boarding school in Ireland?' she asked.

Grace, Louise and I shook our heads.

'Melissa hasn't said anything about it in *weeks*,' said Grace. 'I wonder why?'

'I bet she's sorry now,' said Alice.

'But why?' asked Louise. 'According to Melissa, that school is the greatest place since Malory Towers.'

Alice shrugged.

'I'm not exactly an expert on what makes Melissa tick, but my guess is, she's nervous about going somewhere new on her own. I bet she wishes she was moving on to the local school in September, just like the rest of us.'

I shook my head.

'No way. It's probably just that she thinks she's too good for the rest of us now.'

I was wrong though.

A few days later, I went into the toilets at lunchtime and found Melissa sitting on the floor sobbing. Even though it was Melissa, my worst enemy in the whole world, I couldn't just walk away, pretending I hadn't seen her. Before I knew what I was doing, I went over to her and asked,

'What's wrong?', almost like I really cared.

At first Melissa didn't answer, and I felt a bit stupid for even thinking that she might be human. I decided that maybe she had broken one of her precious fingernails, or perhaps she'd found a split-end in her beautiful golden hair.

Then Melissa looked up at me, and her face was all pale and crumpled-up looking.

'I'm so afraid,' she said.

'Of what?' I asked. I'd always thought that mean people like Melissa were never afraid of anything.

'Of going away to boarding school,' sobbed Melissa.

At first I didn't know what to say. I had a funny feeling that if I was the one crying, Melissa would have run outside to tell all her friends and have a good laugh at how pathetic I was. I couldn't do that to her, though. For the first time ever, I actually felt a little bit sorry for her.

I sat down beside Melissa, because it seemed like the right thing to do. I thought about putting my hand on her shoulder, but that seemed a bit too much, so I put it into my pocket instead.

'But you wanted to go to boarding school,' I said. 'You told everyone that you begged your parents to let you go.'

Melissa sobbed even harder.

'I know I did. But now I've changed my mind, and my parents say I have to go anyway. They've paid the deposit, and booked me in, and so I have to go. And I'm going to be so lonely there. All my friends will be having *soooo* much fun here together, and I'm going to be far away, on my own.'

'But you'll make new friends.'

I wondered if this was true. Melissa did have friends in our class, but every year she seemed to have fewer friends than the year before. Once even Grace and Louise used to be part of her gang, but now they couldn't stand her. And maybe in secondary school, there wouldn't be so many girls who would be fooled by Melissa's fancy clothes and her pretty face. Maybe they would be clever enough to see right through her to the mean person inside.

Maybe there was a way of telling Melissa to be a nicer person, without hurting her feelings, but I couldn't think of the right words. So I just stood up, and spoke quickly like Mum does when she's trying to distract Rosie after a fall.

'Come on,' I said. 'You should wash your face before anyone else comes in. And don't worry. September is ages away. When the time comes, you'll be so excited about the pool, and the hockey pitch with the super-modern surface, you'll soon forget all about us.'

Melissa stood up slowly, and fixed her hair. I pulled a hard, bleach-free, recycled tissue from my pocket. I held it in my hand for a second, knowing that Melissa was only used to pretty, pink, scented tissues.

Would she take the opportunity to mock me, one more time?

Suddenly I realised I didn't care whether Melissa mocked me or not. I wondered why I used to be so afraid of her, always worried about what she'd think about me and my family. Why did her opinion matter so much?

I held the tissue towards her.

'Here,' I said. 'Use this.'

Melissa hesitated for just one second, then she took the tissue, and used it to wipe her eyes. Then she washed her face and followed me outside.

'Thanks, Megan,' she whispered. 'You've been really nice.'

I shrugged.

'It's OK,' I said.

Melissa began to walk slowly over to her friends. As she got closer to them, she began to walk faster, in her usual confident way, and by the time she reached them, she was tossing her hair, just like everything in her world was perfect.

I couldn't wait to find Alice, so I could tell her what had happened.

'Hmm,' she said when I'd finished my story. 'Sounds like our Melissa is human after all.'

I laughed.

'Who would have thought it?' I said.

Alice laughed too, then she stopped and put her hand over her mouth.

'Maybe we shouldn't laugh at her. Sounds like the poor thing was really upset.'

I nodded.

'She was.'

'And maybe it's not her fault that she's so horrible all the time. Maybe her parents never taught her how to be nice.'

I nodded again.

'Yeah, maybe she can't help herself.'

Then I had a really horrible thought.

'Does this mean we have to like Melissa from now on?' I asked.

Alice thought for a minute, then she shook her head.

'Nah. Liking Melissa is a bit too hard. How 'bout we just don't hate her as much any more?'

I grinned.

'That sounds just about right. Now let's go. There's only five minutes of lunchtime left, and remember Miss O'Herlihy has promised us a maths test. It's long division, your favourite.'

'Yuck,' groaned Alice. 'I can't wait for the summer holidays.'

Chapter twenty-seven

A few weeks later, we had our sixth-class graduation ceremony. It was *totally* brilliant.

The whole school came to watch, and so did our parents and smaller brothers and sisters. Most of us wore our Confirmation clothes. Melissa, of course, had to be different.

'Look at her,' said Alice as soon as she saw her. 'That dress is even uglier than the one she had for her Confirmation. I didn't think that was possible. Where on earth did she find it?'

I put on a posh voice.

'A *veeery* fancy designer store in Paris. She—'

Suddenly Alice put up her hand to stop me.

'We forgot,' she said. 'We're supposed to feel sorry for Melissa. We're not supposed to mock her any more, remember?'

I sighed. It's very hard to stop hating someone when you've been doing it for almost eight years.

Just then, Melissa walked by, wobbling on her very high heels. I smiled at her, and Alice even managed to say,

'You look lovely Melissa,' without smirking or laughing or anything.

At eleven o'clock, we all went into the hall, and it took ages for everyone to settle down. The infants looked tiny, all sitting cross-legged on the floor. I couldn't remember Alice and me ever being that small. Next year, Rosie would be sitting there, and I was kind of sorry that I wouldn't be there to see it.

At last, when everyone was quiet, the principal made a big, long speech.

'I have to say that this sixth class is a credit to the school,' she said after loads of other boring stuff. 'I really cannot remember a sixth class as talented and wonderful as you boys and girls.'

Everyone clapped and cheered and pretended not to remember that the principal had said the same thing about every sixth class since we were in junior infants.

When she finally sat down, we got to play our tin whistles. (I even managed 'Edelweiss' without a single mistake.) We played for ages, until the juniors were jiggling around from boredom.

After that we all had to stand up in turn and tell everyone what our special memory of the school was. Most of the boys remembered gross stuff like kids wetting themselves or getting sick, but luckily no one mentioned the trip to Fota Island. (Maybe Miss O'Herlihy had warned them when Alice and I weren't there.)

Alice's memory was of when we were in first class, and she knocked over three jars of paint, and I stayed with her all through lunchtime to help her clean up the mess. I was glad she picked a memory that included me, even though I couldn't remember that day at all.

My memory was much more recent. I said how happy I was on Alice's first day back at school after eight months in Dublin.

The last part of the ceremony was the song we had been practising for weeks. It was all about friends. When we got to the bit about friends always being there for each other, Alice grabbed my hand and squeezed it until it really hurt.

We sang the chorus about fifty times, and by the time we were finished most of us were crying. Mostly it was happy-sad kind of tears, but poor Melissa was sobbing like she really meant it. Alice went over and gave her a hug, and Melissa got such a fright she stopped crying.

Afterwards everyone had drinks and cake and then it was time to go. Our whole class was going bowling and then on to the cinema. Alice and I went over to say good-bye to my parents. My mum had red puffy eyes. I should have known she'd be the only totally embarrassing mum who would start crying. I told her I was leaving with the others. Mum grabbed me and hugged me tight like I was leaving for the other end of the earth, instead of for the bowling alley five minutes up the road.

'My little girl,' she said. 'Where on earth did all those years go? It only seems like five minutes since you started here.'

Luckily Rosie pushed in between us saying,

'*I'm* your little girl! Megan's a big girl now.'

Mum smiled and took Rosie up in her arms, and it looked like everything was going to be all right. Just then Miss O'Herlihy came over and said,

'Mr and Mrs Sheehan. You should be proud of Megan. She's a great girl.'

That was enough to start Mum crying again. She stood still like she was going to wait until her tears were making a huge puddle around her feet. I wondered if the school had a safety policy for evacuating the school if it gets flooded by tears.

Luckily Dad stepped in and saved me from total embarrassment. He put his arm around Mum and said,

'Come on, you soppy old thing. Let's go home and have a nice cup of tea.'

So they went off arm in arm, and it wasn't that embarrassing at all – as long as you didn't look too closely.

Then we went to say goodbye to Alice's parents. They were standing in a corner discussing where Jamie and Alice were going to stay that night. They both hugged Alice, and then they went off in different directions, like they hardly knew each other. Suddenly my parents didn't embarrass me after all. Watching Peter and Veronica was worse – much, much worse.

Alice and I watched them until they were

gone. Then I turned to her.

'You OK?'

She nodded.

'It's not perfect, but it's OK.'

'Are you sure?' I asked.

She nodded again.

'Sure I'm sure. This is the way my life is going to be from now on. It's taken a while, but at last I'm fine with this.'

I smiled at her.

'I'm not trying to be mean, Alice,' I said. 'But you've said that once or twice before.'

She looked at me with her eyes wide open.

'Once or twice?' she said.

'OK,' I laughed. 'I was trying to be nice. The truth is, you've said it lots and lots of times.'

Alice smiled.

'I was just saying it all those other times. You know, like if I said it often enough, I might end up actually believing it. But I always had a secret hope that Mum and Dad would try again.'

'And now? I asked.

Alice didn't say anything for a minute. Then she spoke very quietly.

'Now I know it's over between them forever,' she said. 'Now I'm ready to move on.'

For the first time ever, I really, really believed her.

I hugged her.

'I am so, so glad for you.'

She hugged me back.

'Trust me. I'm glad too.'

'So no more plotting and scheming?'

She pulled away from me and made a face.

'Hey, I'm just OK with the Mum and Dad thing. I'm not promising anything else. Remember, life's no fun if you don't have secret plans.'

I nodded slowly.

'Yeah. Whatever.'

Then Alice grabbed my arm.

'Now, come on, or we'll be late for the bowling.'

So I waved goodbye to my old school forever, and I ran out on to the street after my very best friend.

COMING SOON

ALICE IN THE MIDDLE

BY JUDI CURTIN

Megan can't *wait* to go away to Summer Camp with her best friend Alice. It will be fantastic — no organic porridge, no school, nothing but fun.

But when Alice makes friends with Hazel, Megan begins to feel left out. Is Megan going to lose her very best friend?

Alice in the Middle by Judi Curtin, autumn 2007

ISBN: 978-1-87471-038-5